Open Skies

Yolande Kleinn

Published by Yolande Kleinn, 2024

www.yolandekleinn.com

Open Skies
By Yolande Kleinn

Cover Design: Yolande Kleinn
Cover Photo: Jeremy Thomas
Cover Font: Engebrechtre from Typodermic Fonts
Interior Font: Born from thehungryjpeg.com

Third Edition January 2024

Print ISBN 978-1-946316-39-4
Digital ISBN 978-1-946316-14-1

For Betsy, who never lets me down.

CHAPTER ONE

"I have it on unimpeachable authority that you two can find anything." Eleazar Dantes spoke with a gruff voice, deeper than his short stature might suggest. For all that he was stocky around the middle, there was something delicate about the deeply lined contours of his face, and his suit might have cost more than a year's rent for the office they were sitting in now.

Dantes had introduced himself imperiously, and Kai believed the name was genuine, not least because he'd heard it before. Beyond that, despite the fact that Dantes was clearly human, Kai had trouble getting a read. He knew Eleazar Dantes by reputation, but he couldn't decide what to make of the man as a prospective client.

Kai glanced to his left, eyes seeking his partner. Ilsa perched on the edge of the only desk in the cramped office. Her face, sienna dark with even deeper freckles, held a practiced blank. But Kai recognized the twitch of her left pinky finger atop her knee: a subtle signal of distrust.

Kai shifted his weight and returned his attention to Dantes. The uncomfortable chair creaked beneath him in protest. Dantes sat in a similar chair, but he didn't look the least bit irritated at the rickety metal edges or the hard back. There was patience in the carbon gray of Dantes's eyes, and his gaze slipped back and forth between Kai and Ilsa. His focus finally settled on Ilsa and her easy perch.

"Miss Vance." Dantes spoke with calm determination, leaning forward to emphasize the subtle plea in his voice. "Whatever concerns you might harbor, I give you my word they are baseless. I'm willing to pay up front for any expenses you might incur on my behalf, and if you're successful, I will double your usual fee."

Rather than reassuring, the generous offer gave Kai pause. And though Ilsa's face showed no outward sign, he knew it had tripped her instincts just as soundly as his own. Their fees were imposing to begin with. For a potential client to offer double wasn't simply unusual: it was potentially dangerous. Whatever Eleazar Dantes intended them to find, he wanted it with a desperation that straightened Kai's spine in alarm. He and Ilsa were a competent partnership—*Vance & Othen, Professional Finders* had built themselves an impressive reputation—but any customer intent on overpaying was best approached with caution.

"We can't accept your contract if we don't know what you're looking for." Ilsa's steady tone gave nothing away. She folded her hands together over her crossed legs and rested twined fingers atop navy-blue dress pants. There was nothing but reassurance in her voice when she continued, "There's no need to be cagey with us, Mr. Dantes. My partner and I understand the importance of discretion. Whether or not we agree to take your case, nothing you say will leave this room."

Gray eyes cut away from Ilsa and skated sideways, catching Kai with piercing weight. "Is that true, Mr. Othen?" Dantes peered intently at him. "Will you guard my secrets as if they were your own?"

"Would your unimpeachable authority have recommended us otherwise?" Kai raised one eyebrow but kept his expression bland. He had nothing to prove to Eleazar Dantes. He certainly wasn't going to defend his own discretion to a man who had already traveled seventy parsecs to offer them double their usual rate. He held himself perfectly still beneath the pointed inspection, waiting out the scrutiny with practiced patience.

If Dantes intended to discomfit a reaction out of Kai, he was going to be profoundly disappointed.

After several awkward seconds, Dantes nodded in quiet satisfaction. "Very well." There was dismissal in the casual shift of his glance as Dantes looked once more to Ilsa. His brow creased deeply beneath the curl of black-and-silver bangs, and his voice fell painfully somber. "I'm looking for my daughter."

Ilsa's brows rose with surprise, and her eyes darted briefly toward Kai before she echoed, "Your daughter."

Kai shared her surprise, though the startlement faded quickly. It wasn't their standard gig: usually they were hired to track down lost valuables, stolen property, even pets in one memorable instance. But he and Ilsa had certainly been hired to find people before, usually family members scattered during the ugliest years of the war.

War was a rending force. Even now, three years since the Enriu had been driven away for good, there still stood deep swathes of scar tissue across entire quadrants. Kai Othen and Ilsa Vance had been approached a handful of times to search for missing loved ones, nearly always by people who could never hope to pay their baseline expenses, let alone their steep commission fees. It was a point of perfect understanding within their partnership that Kai and Ilsa never turned those cases away.

There were some jobs they took on, not for the sake of money, but because it was the right thing to do. If it put a strain on their resources between paying gigs, Kai and Ilsa both agreed it was a worthwhile price for a clean conscience.

They had never been approached by the likes of Eleazar Dantes. Surely a businessman recognized throughout the halls of galactic commerce must possess better resources. Law enforcement, private detectives, employees answerable only to him—local talent he could hire without putting himself in harm's way. Travel in some sectors was still dangerous, peacetime or not. Surely it was even more so for such a prominent figure. Eleazar Dantes had been rich even before the war. In the years that followed, he had proven himself a mastermind at wartime economics and had come through the conflict with unimaginable wealth.

A man who profited off of violence and death would have enemies to spare. He must have been desperate indeed to travel so far, alone and in person, to put his case before Kai and Ilsa now.

"Her name is Abigail." Dantes pulled a small data screen from an inside pocket of his gray coat. He tapped an indecipherable sequence into the screen, summoning the relevant data, then handed it to Ilsa.

Ilsa peered at the information with assessing eyes. If their current office were equipped with all the standard technological niceties, she could have projected whatever she was seeing so that Kai could peruse simultaneously. But this was a shit building in an even shittier port town—their last real paycheck was beginning to fade uncomfortably far behind them—and Kai had to settle for waiting his turn. Eventually Ilsa handed the small data screen over, and Kai leaned forward to accept it.

Instead of the list of dates and information he expected, Kai found himself greeted by the image of a woman's face. She was young, in her mid-twenties if he had to guess, and she wore her hair in a thick braid that twined forward over one shoulder. She wasn't smiling. Defiance tightened both the line of her jaw and the set of her shoulders, giving her an air of fierce determination.

Kai liked her already.

"Abigail Dantes?" Paternity was hardly a guarantee that the woman shared her father's name.

"Yes." Dantes took the screen back and tapped it dark, then put the device away. "She'll be thirty this year, if she's still alive." A cloud passed across Dantes's face, an expression both shadowed and ferocious, and Kai found himself sympathizing despite his suspicious nature. He hadn't seen his own family face-to-face since long before the war, but he could well imagine the anxiety he would feel at not knowing they were all right.

"And you've tried to find her before?" Kai pressed. He pretended not to notice the quick glance Dantes cast toward Ilsa. It was a fleeting look, obvious confusion at the fact that Ilsa seemed content to allow the questions to progress without participating. A familiar expression, to be sure. Kai knew full well how he and Ilsa appeared to strangers. Between the two of them, Ilsa seemed the more collected and serious, more intelligent. Her composed demeanor and professional attire made people assume she was in charge, especially when contrasted with Kai's brawnier figure and more casual dress. Dark trousers, faded shirt, worn leather jacket, stubbled jaw: he looked more like a bodyguard than a business partner, and he had certainly used people's prejudices to his own advantage in the past. It was good to be underestimated in his line of work.

But there was no point misleading a man who clearly hoped to be their client by the end of this interview. There was no reason to hide the fact that Kai and Ilsa shared a more balanced arrangement than superficial judgments might suppose. Ilsa preferred to listen; Kai preferred to talk. They both had their strengths. Kai's just happened to lie in the realm of human interaction. If they were genuinely considering this proposal, then Kai would damn well conduct the interview his own way.

To his credit, Dantes recovered quickly from his hesitation, and turned to address Kai directly. "I've hired half a dozen private investigators in the past three years. Every single one of them has reported back with resounding failure. They've all tried to convince me my daughter can't be found." Dantes paused and drew a deliberate breath, visibly steadying himself. "I sent her into hiding during the war, for her own protection."

Kai kept his eyes on Dantes's distressed face, but the eyebrow he arched was all for Ilsa. "Why did you need to protect her?"

Dantes's expression cleared, and he huffed a quiet, ugly laugh that managed to sound angry and exhausted and wounded all at once. "I was... not a popular figure, as you can well imagine. My unexpected success during troubled times earned me a veritable army of enemies, many of whom still plague me to this day." Stubborn pride seemed to straighten Dantes's spine, despite the fact that his posture was perfect to begin with. "I will not apologize for seizing opportunities that were rightfully mine to take. But I also couldn't allow my notoriety to put my daughter in danger. I was besieged on all sides. I trusted no one, least of all my employees, and I needed to know she was safe."

The explanation seemed perfectly reasonable. It sounded honest and hurt and painfully sincere. But it also sounded incomplete. There was something guarded behind Dantes's stiff-backed pride.

Kai straightened in his chair, consciously matching the man's rigid posture. "Was there someone specific you needed to protect her from?" Dantes's eyes narrowed with displeasure, but before he could protest, Kai pressed, "Mr. Dantes, if you aren't candid with us, there's no way we can accept your commission."

Dantes's face was a practiced blank, but Kai still perceived an internal struggle in the delay, not to mention the faint crease that flickered at the center of his brow. Whatever was giving him pause, Kai sensed it nearly sending Dantes into retreat despite the distress that had brought him all this distance.

A moment later, Dantes's tension visibly, if reluctantly, eased. He still sat straight in the uncomfortable chair, but there was new resignation in the line of his shoulders. "It's private. A family matter that I have gone to great lengths to keep from the public eye."

Kai waited with deliberate patience. He didn't need to glance at Ilsa to convince her to do the same.

Grudgingly, with visible discomfort and no hint of his previous poker face, Dantes answered, "Helena Kanne."

Kai blinked. "I don't know who that is."

"I suppose you wouldn't. She's my late wife's only sister."

"And you think she's a danger to Abigail?" Kai's brow furrowed. "Why?"

A fresh look of discomfort colored Dantes's expression, but this time he didn't hesitate. "I don't like to cast aspersions when I have no proof. Please know these are only suspicions; if I had more, I'd have taken action years ago." A pause, a cut of his eyes from Kai to Ilsa and back again, and then Dantes continued, "My wife's death was no accident. And while I could never prove anything—I could never find a tangible *motive*, let alone evidence—I know just how few people Lora let close. Helena was one of only a handful of suspects, and her relationship with Lora was... complicated."

"Was Helena Kanne's relationship with Abigail also complicated?"

"They were never close," Dantes said. "And *all* I have are suspicions. I can't imagine a reason Helena would want to hurt Abigail. But I couldn't have imagined losing my wife, either. It was just one more reason to get my daughter safely out of sight. The war made such a mess, even for me. I couldn't protect her any other way."

Kai wanted to press for more detail, but some kinder instinct stopped him. There was uncanny certainty in Dantes's tone. For all his care not to claim sure answers, Dantes had the air of a man with no doubts at all. He didn't just suspect his sister-in-law; he *knew* who was to blame for his wife's death. Much as Kai wanted more to go on, he sensed Dantes shutting down around the painful topic.

Kai hesitated. He spoke his next words with strenuous care. "Mr. Dantes... The war has been over for three years. Even the most damaged systems within the Alliance have managed to repair basic communication capabilities. Surely Abigail should have been in touch with you by now."

"Exactly." Dantes leaned forward in his chair. Determination glinted in his eyes as he glanced back and forth between Kai and Ilsa. "She *should* have contacted me by now. But she hasn't. What if she can't? What if she's hurt or lost? What if she's in trouble?"

"She could be dead," Ilsa said softly. Kai stiffened, glaring in rebuke at her clumsy observation. Ilsa's eyes widened for the briefest instant as she realized she'd spoken aloud—that she'd spoken unkindly—and then Kai turned away to find steel on Eleazar Dantes's face.

"I refuse to believe it." The assertion came out a dangerous growl. "Until I see a body, Abigail is alive and healthy. If she were dead, there would have been something to find before now."

Kai wasn't so sure, but it would be cruel to argue otherwise. With even greater care, he asked, "Is it possible she doesn't want to be found? Perhaps she's still hiding from Helena Kanne."

A strange look passed over Dantes's face at the suggestion, unreadable shadows and a fleeting grimace. There was something stern, almost accusatory, in his voice when he snapped, "Abigail would *never* do that to me. She would find a way to contact me if she could. My daughter is no coward. She wouldn't leave me to suffer this eternal doubt." Then, obviously reluctant to concede the point but recognizing the validity of the question, he added, "Even if she would, it doesn't change anything. I still need to see her. I need to know she's okay."

Silence closed in through the claustrophobic office, heavy and stifling in the too-warm air. Kai looked to Ilsa again, not in rebuke this time but in question. He could feel Dantes watching them. The pleading weight of the man's regard echoed heavily in the quiet, no matter that Kai wasn't looking at Dantes.

Kai pressed his mouth into a thin line, turned his head a fraction, but otherwise held perfectly still. Ilsa met his eyes. Her own gaze narrowed almost imperceptibly, and Kai knew they were in complete agreement. Wary of Eleazar Dantes, unsure of him, but firmly convinced of his frank desperation. They had never refused to search for missing family before. They certainly couldn't do so in good conscience now, especially with double their usual fee on the table.

It was Ilsa who turned to Dantes and said, "We'll take your case. Will you sign our standard contract?"

"Of course." Dantes nodded. "But with one particular request."

Kai felt his own eyebrows rise high on his face, but he gestured for Dantes to continue.

Dantes looked far too sure of himself as he explained, "I want to accompany you in your search. I want to be there every step of the way."

Ilsa blinked, and her large eyes looked owlish with dubious surprise. "You're joking."

Dantes shook his head. "I've never been a jesting man. I assure you, I am entirely in earnest."

"It's dangerous enough for you *here*," Ilsa protested, and this time her unguarded words were a sentiment with which Kai fervently agreed. "Your name isn't a popular one, and our investigation is liable to tread through even less sympathetic sectors. It's not safe. You can't very well pack along a bodyguard on a trip like this."

"I don't care." Dantes met their skepticism with level stubbornness. "Either I go with you, or the entire deal is off."

"We're not fond of ultimatums," Kai said softly. He was impressed despite himself when Dantes held fast, stubbornly refusing to back down.

"We're talking about my baby girl," Dantes said. "I have no intention of making a nuisance of myself. And I'll increase my offer if that's what it takes. But I *will* accompany your investigation."

Kai exchanged a quick glance with Ilsa, but Dantes's tone had already decided him. He was relieved to find silent assent in his partner's implacable expression.

"Fine," Kai relented. "But *we* make the travel arrangements. And if you aren't ready to leave by morning, we'll depart without you. Understood?"

"Understood." Dantes visibly relaxed with the concession. "Now. Where is this contract you need me to sign?"

"I'll draw it up for you tonight." Ilsa rose from the edge of the desk. Kai stood as well, leaving Dantes no choice but to follow suit. Simple as it would have been to revise their standard contract and sign it before Dantes departed the office, neither Kai nor Ilsa offered. There were certain steps they needed to take before obligating themselves in writing.

"Well." Dantes straightened. "I'll expect your missive. Where shall I meet you in the morning?"

"We'll send you the details along with the contract," Kai said, and escorted him to the door.

*

Ilsa kept an apartment not far from the office she shared with Kai, and six blocks' distance made for a dramatic change of scenery. The neighborhood where she lodged wouldn't be anyone's idea of a holiday destination, but it was cleaner and better lit than the industrial district that abutted it. The buildings stood just as tightly packed, but as Ilsa approached her destination, the architecture changed, a tangible shift away from lumpy stonework and rusted industrial frames. Cardim Lane boasted sleeker edges and sharper skylines. Windows glinted not just with reflected sunlight but with active security panes, and the few shops and kiosks conducted their business with dated but functional tech.

There was still a crust of age and disrepair dulling every surface, settling across the streets with subtle determination. But this far from the landing hubs, there was significantly less grime. The air didn't carry such an overwhelming smell of engine grease and toxic discharge. Port cities weren't always unpleasant, but Naius V had proven one of the most uninviting planets Ilsa and Kai had landed on yet.

She let herself into a looming building that looked exactly like the structures to either side, then navigated a long hall with severely high ceilings. Her apartment was on the sixteenth floor, reached by a quick ride up a shuddering lift. The rental was more like a cramped bedroom than a proper home, but it was clean and secure. The fact that the back wall—the one facing toward the central port terminal and landing hubs—was ninety-percent window made up for a great deal of inconvenience.

Ilsa harbored a fondness for spacecraft. The reality of space travel might have proved more tedious than the romantic imaginings of her childhood, but that fact didn't stop her from appreciating the sleek lines of a well-designed ship. It sure as hell didn't prevent her enjoying the way heat shuddered visibly around descent thrusters as atmosphere-competent vessels made their landings and liftoffs. One planet or a hundred, the view never lost its appeal.

Overhead lights activated as she stepped across the threshold and into her apartment. She would have a little over an hour before Kai appeared on her doorstep, but that should be more than enough time. Her desk was a mess of data screens and tools, and Ilsa sat to begin her work. She ignored the question of Dantes's contract for the moment, focusing her efforts elsewhere. Research first. There were things she needed to know about Eleazar Dantes before she and Kai signed themselves over to his employ.

An hour later she had what she needed, and Ilsa turned her attention to packing. Her sturdy rucksack held nearly everything she owned, and the rest she would leave behind without regret. Ilsa lived light, traveled light, and kept few possessions beyond her clothes and equipment. It was part instinct, part conscious choice; there was no point accumulating volumes of trivial effects when a new transport ship hovered just beyond every horizon.

Ilsa knew from experience that even if Eleazar Dantes hadn't called them away from Naius V, she would have been too restless to stay put much longer. Funds had grown tight, but they weren't a problem just yet. This was nowhere near the longest she and Kai had gone between jobs in their seven years as partners. But Ilsa could feel the streets and walls constricting around her as the surrounding city grew too familiar. This place was becoming routine, and Ilsa couldn't bear the mounting itch the sense of familiarity put beneath her skin.

No matter how predictable her need to board a ship for elsewhere, Kai always followed without complaint. His willingness to uproot at a whim was a vital tenet of their partnership. It was also an unspoken understanding, and one Ilsa depended on more than she would ever admit. Few friendships were stubborn enough to survive through a lifetime of wanderlust, and Ilsa could hardly blame the friends who had faded and flagged along the way. Keeping up with her was a lot to ask.

Kai did it without the need of asking. Loyalty like that was a gift Ilsa never quite knew what to do with.

When her door slid open without warning, Ilsa didn't startle at the sound. Caution made her turn quickly, but a glance only confirmed what she already knew: Kai had arrived right on schedule. Ilsa was well accustomed to him entering her space unannounced. She'd given over her pass codes on day one planet-side, as she did in every new location, and she offered a humoring smile as Kai strode across the threshold into her apartment.

Kai shrugged off his jacket, looking out of place in the tiny room. He stood almost a foot taller than Ilsa, and his broad shoulders took up a comedic amount of space amid the narrow walls and sparse furniture. With his sturdy frame and bulky muscle, he looked very much like he might shatter the impractical little chairs beside what passed for a kitchen table. Ilsa pursed her lips to hide her amusement as Kai strode past the ridiculous chairs, dropping his jacket over one of them on his way. He planted his feet before the enormous window instead. The sun was setting at the edge of a polluted sky, and the result was a horizon painted violently in orange and red and pink. Clouds scattered through the mess like an afterthought. The city below looked garish in the skewed sunlight.

For all its gaudiness, Ilsa found it a beautiful view. It was one of the few things she would miss about Naius V.

"I see you're already packed," Kai said without taking his eyes off the horizon. He stood completely at ease, his posture loose, his hands stuffed carelessly in his pockets. His rust-and-copper hair was cropped particularly short at the moment. Backlit by the setting sun, it looked eerily like a sheen of fire across his scalp.

Ilsa moved to join him, and they stood shoulder to shoulder. She crossed her arms over her chest and considered the disjointed city stretching into the distance below. Despite the view, she wouldn't be at all sorry to go.

"Have you begun a data trace on Abigail?" Kai asked, glancing down at her with green-hazel eyes.

"Yes. As much as I can from here. Nothing I found changes tomorrow's itinerary."

Dantes had given them everything he knew about his daughter's last known physical location. Wherever she'd gone after that, Kai and Ilsa's search could begin in only one place.

Ilsa was familiar with Corriah Mor. An independent space station, it stood brazenly at the intersection of seven different Alliance trade sectors. It was the nearest port of its size, and the largest that was still intact from before the war. It was also the only place within a dozen parsecs that had direct access to all the data streams Ilsa would need to patch into. That it happened to be the only physical clue Dantes could provide toward his daughter's whereabouts was too logical to be coincidence. A journey to disappear had to begin somewhere, and what better place for Abigail to lose herself than Corriah Mor?

"What about Eleazar Dantes?" Kai asked. His posture hadn't changed, but he shifted so that his attention was fully on Ilsa rather than the city below. He needed a shave, but she had no intention of telling him so. He seemed to favor the stubble, especially when they traveled, and he would certainly blend in better if he looked a little rough around the edges.

"Everything I found fits with the information he volunteered." Ilsa paused and added a wry, "More or less. You won't be surprised to learn he took some editorial liberties."

"What kind of liberties?"

"He was right that his wife's death was no accident. The local authorities agreed—they tried to charge Dantes himself with her murder." She ignored Kai gawping at her and continued, "The charges were ultimately dismissed, so I had to break into some sealed court documents to get the full story. From what I can tell, they simply lacked the evidence to convict. Which... of course they did. Can't produce evidence that isn't *there.* Dantes's defense did implicate Helena Kanne, but it doesn't look like anyone pursued the investigation after his acquittal."

Kai whistled, long and low. "Sounds ugly as hell."

"No kidding." Ilsa shook her head. "It's no wonder he didn't want to give us details. And get this: I tried to track down Helena Kanne? I can't find recent traces of her *anywhere*. She fell off the map after Dantes's trial. There were some hiccups in the system at first—if I had to guess, I'd say she was traveling and trying to keep a low profile—but nothing since."

"That's a little suspicious."

"A little," Ilsa snorted. "We'll have to move carefully. If she's still watching, we could end up leading her straight to Abigail Dantes.

"We'll stay vigilant." Kai's expression softened into a look of fond familiarity. "There's something else bothering you about all this."

Ilsa breathed a quiet sigh, but she waved a dismissive hand as the tension eased from her shoulders. "I just don't like that he's coming along. We're not babysitters. How the fuck does Dantes expect us to do our job *and* keep him out of trouble?"

"He doesn't," Kai reminded her. "His safety's on his own head. We'll add a waiver clause to the contract if we have to, but our job begins and ends with the investigation." Then, after a pause, Kai asked, "What do you make of *him*?"

Ilsa huffed and scrutinized the horizon to keep from rolling her eyes. "I don't know." People weren't exactly her bag of tricks. She preferred computers to flesh-and-blood puzzles. There were reasons she and Kai tended to divide responsibilities the way they did. "What do *you* think of him?"

Kai shrugged. "I think he genuinely wants to find his daughter. And I think he'll keep his head down, at least. Hopefully he'll stay out of the way, let us do our job without interference." Kai's next words were quiet. "He's desperate. He wouldn't be here otherwise."

"Do we trust him?" Ilsa was confident of the answer, but she wanted to hear Kai say it just the same.

"We're too smart to trust him." Kai spoke with only a trace of worry, the words softened by a teasing smile. "But we can at least rely on him to pay."

"Come on, then." Ilsa nudged Kai with one elbow and turned from the window. "You can book tomorrow's transport while I draft this contract. The sooner we get moving, the better I'll feel."

CHAPTER TWO

Kai bought passage on a massive passenger liner scheduled for direct transit to Corriah Mor. Three days was the shortest possible duration for the journey, but at least the trip looked set to pass more comfortably than anticipated. He'd been braced to share cramped fourth-class bunks the entire distance; those were the best accommodations they could secure on short notice. But with Dantes along for the ride, they'd been upgraded to larger cabins before even setting foot aboard ship. Three separate berths. Not first class as Kai suspected Dantes wanted, or even commerce class since those were already overbooked, but still an improvement for which Kai was grateful.

"You could have upgraded only yourself," he pointed out to Dantes as they followed an attendant through the enormous ship. The attendant was roughly human-sized, stout and bipedal. From the scaly patterns that marked his visible skin, Kai guessed he was from somewhere near the Setrius Cluster. When Dantes didn't respond to his pointed comment, Kai continued, "Ilsa and I would have found you at the receiving dock, no trouble." They were well accustomed to tight travel arrangements, and three days was hardly long enough to lose track of their client entirely, even on a vessel as large as this one.

Dantes scowled as though Kai had just said something crude. "Don't be absurd. I've contracted you to do me a valuable service. I won't have my employees traveling in squalor."

Dantes's words were cutting, and not at all a fair appraisal. The fourth-class cabins may have been cramped and confining, barely larger than the narrow bunks that populated them, but they were every bit as clean and functional as the rest of the ship. Corriah Mor was a megacenter of travel and commerce. Even departing from a nowhere port like Naius V, there were plenty of legitimately licensed vessels to choose from.

Kai didn't bother calling out the blatant fallacy, but from his other side, Ilsa pointed out, "We're more like private contractors than we are employees." Kai threw her a wry look that made Ilsa's eyebrows rise, but she fell silent. Kai quieted too, leery of talking Dantes out of paying for a full set of fancier accommodations.

The corridor grew busier with every step, though the crowd was still nothing like the crush of bodies that would be settling into the cheaper zones below. The figures hurrying past were mostly human—Naius V was a Terran settlement first and foremost—but Kai spotted a handful of other species along the way. As he followed the stern attendant, threading a steady path through the bustle, he caught fleeting glimpses of fur and scales and leathery limbs, even feathers for a brief moment.

The three rooms were located nowhere near each other, and Dantes clearly found the fact distasteful. Perhaps he didn't trust Kai and Ilsa any further than they trusted him. Perhaps he wanted to keep even closer tabs than Kai had realized. Surely Eleazar Dantes was a man accustomed to closely protecting his investments.

But even a rich and powerful businessman didn't have the clout to oust other travelers from rooms that had already been paid for. Maybe nearer his own solar system he could have swung his weight around to greater effect, but it seemed Naius V was too far out of range to respect Dantes's financial influence.

When they reached the first of their three stops—Dantes's room—Kai paused at a firm hand on the shoulder.

"Mr. Othen." Dantes spoke quietly enough that Kai had to strain to hear the words in the noisy corridor. "I trust you will inform me if you discover anything useful while we are en route to Corriah Mor." It wasn't a question, and though the hushed tone fell somewhere short of command, Kai still understood the sober weight of the request.

"Of course." He doubted Ilsa would learn more mid-trip than she'd been able to glean from her home terminal the night before, but it was always possible. Kai saw no point in refusing a request far more reasonable than Dantes's insistence on accompanying them in the first place.

Dantes nodded, released him, and retreated through the door into his cabin. Through the portal, Kai caught a glimpse of a single room with generous dimensions. Of course there were no windows. Kai spotted a proper bed, though, just before their stout guide urged them impatiently forward. Kai settled once more into step beside Ilsa, and they followed obediently past several corners, through corridors that seemed to vary constantly—broader, taller, narrower than the halls before—but never constricted far enough to prevent Kai and Ilsa moving easily side-by-side.

They traveled what felt like an enormous distance before finally halting at a door that looked exactly the same as the rest.

"Here is sir's room," the sober attendant announced, but he was looking at Ilsa, and it was to her he handed the small rod that would unlock the security seal. She accepted the device, palming it as she gave a polite smile and a dip that wouldn't have passed for a curtsy in any sector Kai had visited.

Then she turned to Kai, and there was eloquent caution on her face. Her appearance was severe in the long coat she favored for traveling. The dark, heavy fabric reached nearly to her knees, revealing sturdy trousers and tall boots that made her look as ready to hike rough terrain as ride in style through the stars.

"Find me when you're settled?" She waved the security rod in front of the sensor panel, and the door slid smoothly open. "Or would you rather I come to you?"

"I suspect Dantes will hunt us *both* down before you get the chance," Kai observed dryly, "but I'll find you."

"Come, come," the attendant interrupted, urging him to follow. Kai cast one last look over his shoulder and saw Ilsa disappear into her room, her oversized rucksack bumping against the doorframe.

"Quickly please, sir," his guide admonished. "This way."

Kai shrugged his own bag higher onto his shoulder and followed without a word.

*

Ilsa knew what the exterior of Corriah Mor looked like solely from archival images. While she'd been to the station before, she had never traveled in the kind of luxury that might allow a glimpse. Even this trip, with Dantes's insistence on upgrading their shipboard quarters, she didn't have access to those few observation decks open to civilians with the priciest boarding passes.

She'd never been fond of the claustrophobic confines of space travel. They may have been the necessary trade-off to her nigh-constant wanderlust, but the price was a steep one.

Ilsa had learned early in their acquaintance that Kai didn't share her distaste. He seemed as easy in the cramped, windowless hold of a cargo dispatch as he did on the sturdier surface of moons and planets. More than once he had suggested they stage their between-commission headquarters aboard a high-traffic space station. They could be at the center of everything, perfectly placed to catch the edges of mobile commerce, not to mention an unlimited stream of potential clients with dreams of lost treasure.

There was nothing unreasonable in Kai's suggestion, but Ilsa always shot him down. At the beginning she would cite the high rents that came when space was at a premium. But she and Kai had learned each other too well since those early days. A lie, even one so silly and harmless, couldn't continue to fool her partner, and Ilsa had ultimately—sheepishly—admitted the truth. She needed ground and sky. Weather and wind and proper air, not oxygen filtered through reclamation systems until it smelled more of metal than of anything green.

Their layovers between clients could last weeks, sometimes months at a time. A short span of days in space invariably made Ilsa feel antsy and wrong in her own skin. She hated to think what several weeks might do.

Now, despite the lack of viewports to show progress, Ilsa knew their passenger liner was mooring alongside Corriah Mor. She could tell from the minute changes in momentum and gravity, barely discernible shifts that were all the sensation that managed to carry through the ship's powerful inertia buffers. There was a brief but jarring catch as the vessel's main docking ports bracketed themselves to the station.

"All right?" Kai asked quietly, the words only for her. Dantes stood to Kai's other side. They had all three abandoned their bunks in favor of joining the early crowds in the embarkation lounge, surrounded by passengers impatient to exit from ship to station the moment the docking ports slid open.

"Fine," Ilsa answered just as quietly. She hoisted her rucksack more securely over her shoulder. The standard disembarkation announcements filtered over the lounge's speaker system, a repetitive sequence of messages echoed over and over in two dozen different languages. *Wait for the warning lights to deactivate before approaching the portals. Do not step through until all exits are completely open. Mind all guidance panels and security officials. Have customs documents at the ready.* Ilsa understood some half-dozen languages well enough to decipher the instructions and recognized familiar snatches from several more.

She knew Kai had a firm grasp on far more languages than she did, and she wondered if he could decipher the murmur of conversations surrounding them. The majority of the waiting crowd was human, but nearly a quarter of the throng was composed of different species, and Ilsa could make out little of what they were saying.

The exit portals themselves were enormous, each large enough to permit comfortable egress to figures three times the size of an average human. Few races stood tall or wide enough to need such accommodations, but strict regulations mandated the dimensions. Licensed vessels above a certain class had to be equipped for all Alliance passengers. Even in the wake of war, these regulations were strictly enforced. Ilsa felt eclipsed as she watched the intricate metal panels smoothly dilate, allowing the waiting passengers through in a mostly orderly line.

They stepped into an enormous arrivals bay with widely spaced bulkheads and a staggeringly high ceiling. Massive ramps led from the vessel to the bay floor far below, and Kai crowded behind her as Ilsa fell into step with the disembarking crowd. She let her eyes and mind wander as she followed the dull and ceaseless current. Ilsa struggled to keep her attention focused outward on her surroundings, forced herself to pay sharp attention to the rhythm and trudging progress.

It wouldn't do to drop her guard in such an arena. She and Kai were certainly nobody special, and they faced no greater dangers than the clever pickpockets hidden throughout the tight press. But Eleazar Dantes was another matter entirely. His was a face that might be recognized, and a name that certainly would be. Ilsa had done some extra digging on *him* over the course of their journey, and had discovered he was accustomed to traveling with an entourage of attendants and security personnel.

Dantes was alone now, except for Kai and Ilsa. And though they were under no contractual obligation to protect him, they would have little choice if someone took a hostile interest. Helena Kanne was only one potential danger, and Ilsa didn't enjoy unknowns. She didn't much like the exposed feeling that came of knowing Dantes was somewhere at her back.

It took them nearly two hours to navigate all three security checkpoints and enter the station proper. The din was quieter here as fellow travelers dispersed about their business. They reached a smaller corridor than the enormous docking port behind them, but it was still an impressive space, especially when one considered the tightly measured architecture of Corriah Mor. The high ceiling actually slanted upwards far ahead, the natural curve of the station coming visible with distance.

To left and right stood shop fronts and inviting doorways, businesses inviting new arrivals to spend their money on food and fanfare and comfort.

"I reserved lodgings on deck twenty-three," Ilsa announced, loud enough for both Kai and Dantes to hear her over the bustle of commerce. She looked to Kai and found his gaze drifting across the variety of offerings that filled the expansive space.

"Dinner first?" he asked without looking at her.

Ilsa rolled her eyes, though only Dantes seemed to catch the gesture. "You can *bring* me dinner. I have work to do." The sooner she settled in and started digging, the sooner they would have what they needed and could decide their next move. Kai might be content to linger aboard Corriah Mor longer than necessary, but Ilsa had no intention of wasting any extra time.

Kai hit her with an easy grin, clearly untroubled by Ilsa's brusque insistence on getting down to business. He doffed an imaginary hat, then nodded politely to Dantes before retreating into the milling crowd. Ilsa kept easy track of him as he moved farther down the wide corridor. His height and broad shoulders made it easy to track him amid the flurry of activity. When she lost sight of him behind a vendor's cart, she turned at last to Dantes.

"Shall we?" she asked, indicating a different direction. A smaller hall branched off from the main corridor, and as they moved into it, some of the heavy clamor muffled and eased. Dantes kept pace with her as Ilsa navigated several turns that, though unfamiliar, she was confident led in more or less the right direction.

"What happens next?" Dantes moved with casual grace. He carried no luggage except a small case with stiff sides, the handle clasped securely in one hand. His wandering gaze seemed to take in their surroundings with distaste, bland expression not quite blank enough to mask the frown that threatened at one corner of his thin mouth. He looked meticulous and out of place in the dully functional hallway.

Ilsa shrugged her unencumbered shoulder. "Next, I see what I can dig up on the local network and use the station's resources to patch into the wider data stream for the whole sector." She shifted her attention forward. "Kai will start asking around on foot, see if he can find anyone who remembers talking to Abigail when she came through."

Dantes gave a disbelieving start beside her. Neither of them slowed, but Ilsa could feel his stare when he said with obvious skepticism, "That was almost five years ago. Even if Mr. Othen can find someone who was *here*, how can he hope to learn anything about Abigail? For God's sake, there was a war going on. He can't possibly hope to find reliable information."

Impatient ire flared inside Ilsa, alongside an urge to come snappishly to Kai's defense. *She* knew how valuable his contributions were to their efforts—how lost she would be without his practical smarts and people skills—and it irked her when clients tried to dismiss him as simply the brawn of their partnership. Their division of labor was hardly so simple. Kai had brains aplenty in that smugly handsome head of his; and Ilsa might not be the best hand-to-hand fighter the sector had ever seen, but she was damn near a crack shot with the small firearm tucked securely in her pack.

She moderated her tone so that no hint of irritation leaked through. "You'd be surprised. People remember better than you think."

"Hmm," Dantes murmured in reply. It was neither argument nor agreement, and Ilsa let the matter drop.

*

Kai crossed paths with his two travel companions only in passing once they settled in. Their rented quarters were all located in the same narrow hall, and Dantes cornered him to demand updates that very first evening. But despite several hours' extensive legwork, Kai had nothing to report.

The truth was, he hadn't been surprised to come up empty-handed on day one. Kai had a solid system, and he'd spent his first day in the busiest commercial districts of the station. The high-end shops, the expensive restaurants, the well-lit bars and licensed gambling establishments. Tourist centers. The fact that this wasn't his first visit to Corriah Mor didn't change his preferred methods. Kai always began searching in the noisiest neighborhoods before narrowing his field in subtler directions.

He'd known going in how unlikely he was to catch a break the first day. It was a necessary step—he refused to jump ahead and risk missing vital clues—but it was usually futile. There was too much turnover in employment within high-profile businesses. Beyond that, the sheer volume of travelers made it almost impossible for a single face to stand out in the crowd, especially when the face belonged to a woman who'd been doing her damnedest to go unnoticed.

All day Kai had spoken to employees, some human but most not, and all day he'd met with the same brick wall of nothing. *Can't remember. Can't tell you humans apart anyway. Wasn't anywhere near Corriah Mor during the war.* Experience kept him from indulging in the frustration that might have wrapped itself around him otherwise, but Kai could tell Dantes was unimpressed with his report.

"I'll start with the lower decks tomorrow." Kai tried to mask his displeasure at having to explain himself. "If Abigail wanted to maintain a low profile, she'd keep to the less-populated commercial areas." What he didn't bother to explain was that he had significantly higher hopes for tomorrow's efforts. While the lower decks offered a lot more physical ground to cover, they were also slower and quieter, filled with business owners who had long ago settled in for the long haul. Not all of those businesses would have been around five years ago, but plenty were long-term fixtures, with employees who made the station a permanent home. The people working the lower decks were no temporary crowd. They were lifers, aboard Corriah Mor to make a living.

There was still no guarantee anyone would recognize or remember Abigail Dantes, but Kai liked his chances a hell of a lot better.

He got only two or three words out of Ilsa when he stopped by her room with dinner, but there was nothing unusual there, either. Ilsa had patched her own equipment into the room's standard access terminal, spreading screens and amplifiers and encryption nodes across desk and chair and part of the bed. The room was small to begin with, sparse and tidy, but it looked exponentially more cramped with Ilsa's equipment sprawling across every available surface. Even knowing how tightly all that equipment could be packed, it always impressed Kai how much Ilsa insisted on keeping with her, and how efficiently she managed to fit it in the single rucksack she carried. That she also managed to carry a necessary quantity of clothing and travel rations was a marvel Kai had given up on questioning.

There was literally no furniture available for him to sit on—even the bed on which Ilsa perched cross-legged had no space left over—so Kai simply handed off one of the small containers of food and sat himself on the floor. He settled with his back to the wall and his feet propped against the side of the bed, fitting himself into the narrow aisle.

He opened his takeout carton without a word and began to eat in unobtrusive silence.

Kai knew better than to interrupt Ilsa when she had that particular sheen of focus in her eyes. She didn't touch her dinner right away, but Kai went ahead and dug into his own, eating with his fingers for want of utensils. The food was dry—crumbly balls of vegetable matter and some protein he didn't analyze too closely. The Treeme vendor who had sold him the two cartons called them maskail, but they tasted eerily like falafel.

Eventually, without taking her eyes off the screens of rolling data, Ilsa reached for the carton beside her knee. She ate with the kind of distant distraction that spoke of tenuous data trails and a long night ahead. Kai didn't bother waiting around to see if she would eventually surface. He took his leave as silently as he had arrived, pausing at the door to throw a fondly exasperated look over his shoulder.

Ilsa didn't notice him watching her, any more than she had heeded his company while he ate, or his movement as he rose from the floor. She was dressed in dark pants and a loose shirt that hung low at the collar, comfortable attire for stationary work. Her long hair was tied back, giving a clear view of the smooth line of her jaw and the freckles that dotted her dark skin. Her expression was drawn tight in unassailable concentration.

Kai smiled as a warm rush of affection filled his chest. He exited the room without a word.

*

Right from the start, his second day of digging went better than the first. When Kai reached sub-deck six, he found himself in a space he only recognized as a commercial sector by dint of having visited the station once or twice before. It was a dingy neighborhood, rough around the edges. Even the air felt heavier here, weighted with a scent like laundry that had sat too long between cleanings. There were more human businesses here than above. The corridor was lined with restaurants and narrow shops, plus a handful of liquor stores selling wares that weren't exactly brand-advertised or license-approved.

These were establishments where owners kept their own shop fronts and did their own business. A couple of them even recognized Abigail Dantes when Kai showed her picture around.

"Sure, I remember her," said a man—human—whose thin face and small mouth seemed pressed into a permanent leer. "Pretty little thing. Didn't rightly belong in these parts, you could tell just lookin' at 'er. Must be three years back at least."

Kai slipped the picture back into his jacket pocket and asked, "What can you tell me about her?"

"Why you asking?" the man countered, a sheen of interest creeping into his dull expression.

Kai kept his face bland, allowing no hint of eagerness or even curiosity to show through. "Doing a favor for a friend. I'm hoping to discover where she went after she left Corriah Mor. If you don't know anything else, I'll just..." He gestured toward the door of the tiny dive and turned as if to head that way.

"She didn't exactly say much," the proprietor declared before Kai could make good on his bluff. "Came in for food a bunch of times, tried a little too hard to keep 'er head down. I kept an eye on 'er where I could. Nice girl, wouldn't a' wanted to see her robbed or worse."

"And she gave no hint of where she intended to go?"

The proprietor gave a lazy shrug. "Not to me, she didn't. We weren't chums, you see." He hesitated, fell into a considering pause, then added, "She didn't always sit alone, though. Girl kept some interesting company."

"What sort of interesting company?" Kai carefully kept any hint of impatience out of his tone.

The same pointed shrug preceded the shopkeeper's answer. "The sort a person might go to if they needed to disappear but good. Can't go anywhere without the right documents, see. And those documents leave a big, bright trail, don't they? But 'round here there's plenty of folk willing to provide alternatives for the right price."

"She planned on going completely to ground," Kai realized. "She was meeting with local data forgers."

"I'm not saying I know any such thing," the man hedged, but he sounded calm and confident. "I'm just saying she was meeting with some particular faces."

"Do you have any names?" Kai fished in his pocket for the few loose credit chips he was carrying.

But the proprietor shook his head and admitted, "None as'd do you any good. Most of that lot cleared out when the war got too close to the station. There's plenty of shady types to be found hereabouts, don't get me wrong. But none of them's been aboard Corriah Mor anywhere near long enough."

"I see." Kai drew one of the chips from his pocket despite the disappointment. He handed it over, slipping it discreetly into the cafe owner's palm. "Thank you for your time, sir."

The man pocketed the chip, perpetual leer slipping into a stiff attempt at a smile. Then he nodded, indicating the hall outside with the gesture. "You might as well try that Karikeau place just up the way. Gaudy bar with all the green lights out front. Been around even longer than I have, an' I'm sure I saw your little miss go in there a time or two. Usually with that interesting company of hers."

Kai blinked in surprise. "Thank you," he repeated, more genuinely this time, and finally took his leave.

He didn't bother with the handful of establishments that lined the hall between the cafe and the bar in question. Most were restaurants of some variety or other, with offerings that ranged from nauseating odors to scents that might have seemed mouth-watering in a more savory locale. Not everyone digested the same food—not everyone digested food *period*—and a neighborhood like this catered to all.

He knew when he'd reached the right place partly from the unmistakable blocks of lettering on the sign above the door. Kai couldn't read any of the dozen or so written Karikeau languages, but he would recognize their distinctly ornate zigs and swirls anywhere. Even without the sign he'd likely have known this was the place. Green lights indeed. They formed a surreal pattern about the open doorframe and along the facade of the establishment, distinctive pinpoints of light too dim to cast any real illumination down the corridor. Kai didn't linger looking at them, darting instead through the open archway and into the establishment.

The place had a high ceiling and a twining bar that wrapped along two entire walls. Jangling music played just shy of too loud, and a truly impressive array of drinks lined intricate racks behind the bar. Bottles and boxes and cartons and jugs. There was something for every palate.

The lighting in the bar was dimmer than the corridor outside. Dreary shadows clung to booths and tables, effectively hiding private corners, painting the entire place in discretion. There was so little movement in the grim space that at first Kai thought the establishment empty. Only after his eyes adjusted did he realize there were dozens of people crowded into the long, narrow room. Quiet, motionless at their scattered tables, sharing conversations so soft no hint carried above the too-loud music. No one paid him any attention, and Kai made his way to the emptiest end of the bar.

Several minutes passed before the bartender set aside whatever they were working on in the far corner and approached.

The bartender was indeed Karik. Built tall and slim, with a squat face and no neck to speak of. Female, judging by the markings on the pendant-style jewelry adorning a narrow chest. Efficient in her movements despite the overabundance of limbs and joints, the sharp edges comprising her figure. She wore a pale suit with straight skirts, the fabric hanging flat along the smooth lines of her front. Tight sleeves clung past her wrists, and the only skin left visible—if skin was the right word for the elegant patchwork of leathery creases—were her long fingers and the hairless expanse of her head and face.

Large eyes glinted expressively in the dim light as she glided close. Her gaze lowered to settle curiously on Kai.

"Something to drink?" Her voice was a hissing murmur shaped around the human words, putting the question deliberately in his language rather than asking in her own.

Kai had to tilt his head back to meet her eyes. He let gratitude show in his smile—he could blunder his way through some Karikeau dialects but wasn't keen to prove it—and asked, "Gaiminn Whiskey?" Gaiminn whiskey was a tame variant on the Terran standard, a concoction brewed by a people who appreciated the fine flavor but didn't process alcohol especially well. Unable to drink the wide variety of human-brewed whiskeys exported between Alliance worlds, Gaiminn entrepreneurs had perfected their own brewing methods that packed significantly less punch than the original.

"Are you sure you wouldn't prefer something stronger?" the bartender asked, but the faint hint of music shaping the words told him she was teasing. There was no change in her expression as she poured the drink without waiting for his answer, then handed it to him without flourish.

"Thanks." He accepted the glass but didn't yet drink.

The bartender put away the squat bottle of whiskey. Without taking her eyes off of Kai, she leaned her first set of elbows on the bar and crossed the second set in front of her flat chest. "You haven't the look of a man who only wants a drink."

Kai grinned, a quick flash of teeth, and met her gaze. "No. I'm looking for someone."

Her lipless mouth barely moved as she answered, "You've come to the wrong place, then. Corriah Mor is terrible for finding people, and this bar is worse than most."

"Still." Kai took an appreciative sip of the whiskey in his hand, savoring the smoky flavor, the faint burn at the back of his throat. "I'm looking for a human woman. She would have come through here during the war."

Dark fingers tapped a quick rhythm against pale sleeves and then stilled. "That was some time ago." Again there was a melodic hint of humor to the words.

"Years," Kai conceded. Then, pressing his luck, he asked, "How long have you been aboard Corriah Mor?"

She blinked and answered, "Long enough, I think. Have you a picture?"

Kai showed her, holding the image steady. He relinquished it when she unfolded her arms to take it from his hand and stare more closely. Her perpetually still face gave no indication of whether she recognized the human woman, but the fact that she was taking her time about it gave Kai something like hope. Finally she handed the picture back, and Kai tucked it away in his pocket.

"I've memory of this human." She folded her arms once more. "She visited this establishment many times during her stay. I've no knowledge of why she came or why she left."

"How about where she went?" Kai asked softly.

The bartender regarded him in disconcerting silence. She held motionless through several seconds that expanded into one full minute, then two. Finally, she answered, "Somewhere in the T'i

Yara system, I think." When Kai blinked at her in pleased surprise, she explained, "Humans do not always give credit where it is due. Karikeau hearing, for example, is acknowledged to be the best in this quadrant or any other."

Kai made a mental note never to make the same mistake himself. "And did you hear anything else about her destination?"

"No. Your quarry was... circumspect. She was a memorable girl, but I know only that she was running from something dire and in quite a hurry to make her escape."

Of course she was running. Kai thought of Helena Kanne and what little Ilsa had been able to unearth, a faint trail on the move so soon after the death of Lora Dantes. He tried to imagine what it must have been like for Abigail, running from someone who should've had her back. Running from her own family. Briefly—unkindly—Kai considered the shady, ferocious character of Eleazar Dantes and wondered if there were more going on than the man had admitted.

It was a ridiculous question: of course there was more going on than Dantes admitted. But there was also wounded sincerity in Dantes's eyes when he spoke about Abigail. There was feeling in his desperation to find his daughter.

Kai lifted the whiskey glass in a small salute of gratitude. "Thank you. Truly. You've been an enormous help."

The bartender acknowledged his thanks with a gesture somewhere between a bow and a nod, a brief tip of her head and torso, and then retreated down the bar to assist a new customer. Kai drank another slow sip of his whiskey. When he departed, he left a hefty tip along with the credits to cover his tab.

He had the rest of the day before him, and an entire station of potential sources to pin down. As he navigated the corridor the way he'd come, he did his best to ignore the nagging voice at the back of his mind, suggesting he had maxed out his luck for the day and would hit only brick walls from here on out.

*

"It's been two days," Dantes announced, his tone cool. "What have you found?"

Ilsa bit back the instinctive irritation threatening to color her answer. It bothered her that she didn't have more to offer after two entire days aboard station, but she rankled at the impatience in Dantes's words just the same. Ilsa disliked the implication that her efforts weren't good enough, that the failing was somehow hers. Dantes's tone implied that their business on Corriah Mor might already be concluded if Ilsa and Kai were doing their jobs properly.

There was no point explaining to a man like Eleazar Dantes that they could only find information if it was there to be found in the first place. He was far too accustomed to getting his way. Ilsa exchanged a glance with Kai, seated to her left in the small booth. Both of them sat across from Dantes, the restaurant a noisy chaos around them.

"Mostly we've learned that your daughter is damn good at covering her trail." Ilsa was proud of herself for managing to sound wry instead of angry. "I tracked her digital footprints while she was aboard the station itself, but I found nothing out of the ordinary. Food, quarters, necessities. All standard expenses. Whatever else she may have spent money on, she was careful not to leave a digital trail. And when I searched for any outbound transport she might've booked, I hit a wall."

"You couldn't find anything," Dantes guessed. His narrowed eyes made him look distinctly unimpressed.

It took Kai gently stepping on her toes to remind Ilsa that glaring daggers at their employer wasn't the best way to get paid.

She smoothed her expression to something neutral and corrected him. "I found too much. Abigail booked seventeen tickets on transports departing for drastically different destinations. She clearly didn't want to be followed."

"Can't you tell which transport she actually boarded?" Dantes demanded. "Unused tickets must be on record *somewhere*."

"Of course they're on record. But the archives don't help us here. I checked: every ticket she purchased was redeemed to secure passage. Abigail could only have boarded one of those ships, but if she gave the other tickets away then there's no telling which passenger was actually her."

"Her identification documents—" Dantes tried to protest.

"Were never accessed from the departures terminal," Ilsa interrupted smoothly. "She must have left under false documents."

"She did," Kai agreed. He was slouched forward, his crossed arms resting atop the table. "Unfortunately, there's no hope of tracking down whoever sold them to her. That crowd left for greener pastures years ago."

"Meaning we've got nothing." Dantes scowled. Frustration visibly tightened his shoulders beneath the dark suit jacket he insisted on wearing.

To Ilsa's surprise, Kai countered, "We've got a little better than nothing."

She turned to him, brows high. "Have we?"

He wore a serious enough expression, but Ilsa deciphered a gleam of levity in the hazel tint of his eyes. He kept his voice level as he asked her, "Did you find any destinations near T'i Yara?"

Ilsa blinked. "Yes. Just one. Chasper." Chasper was scarcely a moon, a rock circling the inhospitable fourth planet in the T'i Yara solar system. What little commerce had collected on Chasper centered around the constantly expanding mining efforts on the planet below. Chasper itself boasted little except the port, and a crowded colony scattered beneath the atmospheric domes covering the surface of the moon.

Kai nodded, pleased and a little smug. "That's where she went. We should see how soon there's a transport available to take us there."

Ilsa looked that very night, but choices were limited. There was one mercenary vessel, unaccustomed to passengers, departing for Chasper at an ungodly hour the next morning. The captain, a surly Frith with a spidery figure and disposition, was willing to lend them a crewmen's bunk in exchange for an unconscionably steep fee.

The next commercial liner bound for the T'i Yara system wouldn't be departing for two weeks, and would arrive on the wrong side of the solar system.

Ilsa booked the crewmen's quarters on the Frith's shabby gundalow, and they were en route with record speed.

"This is unacceptable," Dantes announced on first glimpse of the room they were all three intended to share.

Ilsa silently agreed. She had little problem with the dingy aura of disuse or the hint of rust along the walls. She had certainly traveled in shabbier, dirtier accommodations than this. But the room was minuscule, even by the standards of mercenary space travel, with only a narrow aisle of floor between the bunks. The bunks themselves were long and skinny, nestled directly inside the interior bulkheads like small, uninviting caves. There were only the two bunks, one on each side of the room, which meant someone would need to sleep on the gritty floor or share a bed.

"It's not that big a deal," Kai protested from the doorframe, but even he sounded more tired than convinced. "Anyway, it's too late to make them turn the ship around."

Dantes clearly didn't appreciate Kai's lack of fight. His mouth turned down at the corners and his brow furrowed deeply. He gave off the distinct impression of raised hackles and hardening ire, and Ilsa didn't plan on trying to talk sense into him.

"You think spending *four days* in these... *accommodations* isn't cause for concern?" Dantes growled, glaring about him with obvious disdain. "Fine. You can stay. I'm going to have a word with the captain."

Kai stepped aside as Dantes stormed for the door, allowing him past without protest. The impassive look on Kai's face was belied by the smug glint that made his eyes look more green than hazel. Dantes's angry footsteps faded down the corridor, and Kai stepped fully into the room. The door slid shut with a dull clunk behind him.

"He won't be bribing his way to better arrangements." Ilsa allowed amusement to sneak into the words. "I hacked the crew's roster before we boarded. This is literally the *only* available berth, and they had to rearrange their own sleeping assignments to open it for us in the first place. They don't have any roomier living spaces. Not even for the captain."

Kai grinned and slid the heavy bag from his shoulder, setting it in the corner beside Ilsa's rucksack. "I suppose Dantes will want one of these bunks to himself, then."

"*I'm* sure as hell not sharing with him," Ilsa retorted dryly. "You're certainly welcome to try."

Kai laughed, but ultimately slipped into the bunk behind Ilsa after dimming the overhead lights. It wasn't nighttime according to the ship's arbitrary chronometer, but the unreasonable hour of departure had prevented any of them from sleeping the night before. Ilsa could barely keep her eyes open now that she was settled, and she knew sleep would claim her quickly despite the cool air and the stale odor of the bunk.

Space travel was, by its very nature, chilly. Both Kai and Ilsa slept in multiple layers, but that wasn't always enough. A history of close quarters made their current arrangement familiar, and Ilsa turned onto her side facing the wall of the narrow berth. Kai shifted wordlessly behind her, scooting more securely onto the stiff mattress and trying to get comfortable. He hesitated an extra, inexplicable moment before curling close, but he settled easily once there. His front offered pleasant warmth along Ilsa's spine, fending off the lingering chill. A moment later, his arm slipped around her waist.

Ilsa was rarely one to seek out physical affection, but she enjoyed the uncomplicated warmth of contact when it came unasked. There was an almost tangible feeling of safety in being held this way. Fondness for Kai swelled in her chest, and she listened to the quiet, steady rhythm as his breathing slowed into sleep.

CHAPTER THREE

They reached Chasper at moon-standard midnight. The Frith vessel put down beside the largest of the outpost's several dozen interconnected domes. Kai wished, as fruitlessly as ever, that he could actually *see* the ship approach via steep orbit and finally land on the uninviting rock of the moon's natural ground. As it was, he could faintly imagine the city-sized dome growing larger and larger, overshadowing the cargo vessel until the dome comprised the entire horizon.

The gundalow gave a groaning shudder as its landing struts settled, and audible clangs and pops echoed through the bulkheads. The artificial gravity cut off abruptly, and though expected, the change sent an unpleasant shiver along the length of Kai's spine. He felt too light in his own body now. The moon's natural gravity was barely two-thirds the strength of the artificial system aboard ship, and it pulled even less compared to Naius V so many days behind them.

Seated beside Kai on the edge of their bunk, Ilsa gave no indication that the sudden shift had discomfited her. But Dantes paced near the door, sour expression making it impossible to mistake his feelings on the matter. Kai could sympathize, but still had to quash a rumble of amusement. Dantes's current resemblance to a riled house cat was uncanny, but Kai doubted he would appreciate the comparison.

The dock itself was dead and quiet when they disembarked through the narrow connecting corridors onto solid ground. The only sounds of life came from the crew disembarking simultaneously alongside. Despite a scattering of port staff standing at nearby work stations, there were no echoes of conversation. No one was speaking. The staff members—not a single one of them human—all watched the newcomers with the wary attention of night crew and underpaid security.

The dockside floor was vast and sullen, tinted blue by a glow of safety lights. A dull, steady grind of machinery throbbed through the open space. The section of dome above was startlingly clear, offering a view of midnight sky and a sweeping swathe of unfamiliar stars.

Dantes paid no apparent mind to the view as he strode toward the only occupied arrivals kiosk. Kai meant to follow, but glanced to his left first.

Ilsa had stopped in her tracks and was staring straight up through the transparent dome, taking in the sprawling sky. Calm had begun to relax her shoulders, easing the tightness she'd been carrying since departing Naius V. This shielded arena didn't exactly count as open air, but it was certainly closer than any confined ship or station could offer.

Of course Ilsa was more at ease here; she had her feet on solid ground.

Kai didn't hurry her, though he knew Dantes would grow impatient soon. He simply watched, appreciating the unguarded glimpse, the image Ilsa made in her long coat and tightly braided hair. The moment he started appreciating the smooth line of her throat, Kai forced himself to look away. He glanced ahead of them to where Dantes had concluded his business and now stood waiting with folded arms. Even at this distance, Kai could read a speculative curiosity on Dantes's face, and he reluctantly nudged Ilsa with one elbow.

"Sorry," she murmured. Her face lowered to acknowledge their immediate surroundings. The two fell into step, side-by-side, and joined Dantes at the far end of the dock.

Their accommodations that night were cramped but separate. Kai began his usual routine the very next morning, searching out the nearest commercial establishments before venturing farther into the city. It was difficult—there was far more ground to cover, more distance between shops, more residents and none of them human—but he kept at his questions. He continued stubbornly forward across two, three, four days of determined searching.

No one recognized Abigail Dantes.

Many current residents had been around during the war, and all admitted that plenty of humans passed through back then. But everyone Kai questioned gave some equivalent of a helpless shrug before admitting they really couldn't distinguish one human from the next. They might have seen her. They simply didn't know.

Despite experience reminding him this was a perfectly common setback, Kai still resented having to admit how much *nothing* he'd found when he met Dantes for dinner each night. It didn't help that he was meeting the man alone; Ilsa had buried herself in her own quarters and refused to interrupt her work long enough to emerge.

Kai chose to take this as a good sign. If she were hitting the same unbreakable walls as Kai, she'd have surfaced for respite and distraction by now.

"Miss Vance seems... focused," Dantes observed. It was late evening on the fourth day, and their dinner was uninspired: some kind of fish, spiced heavily in an effort to mask the way transport and reconstitution had leeched it of flavor. The restaurant serving it was pleasant enough, but Kai could tell the place was far beneath Eleazar Dantes's usual tastes.

Kai took a sip of his too-sweet drink. "Ilsa has her own leads to follow. Trust me, it's best to let her work in peace."

"She does this often, then?" Dantes watched Kai with narrowed eyes.

"Often enough." The more honest answer would have been, *only when she's really on to something*, but Kai didn't want to raise Dantes's hopes when he wasn't sure himself just what leads had Ilsa preoccupied. This was isolation more complete than she had required aboard Corriah Mor. She wasn't letting Kai stay when he brought food to her quarters; she insisted she had too much work to do and couldn't abide any distraction.

It was a damn good sign, but Kai had no intention of admitting as much to Dantes.

"Mr. Othen," Dantes said in a tone of studied carelessness. Kai set his drink aside and kept his expression blank as Dantes continued, "I find myself curious, and I hope you won't mind my asking. How did you and Miss Vance come to be partners?"

Considering the clumsiness of Dantes's feigned nonchalance, Kai was relieved to be facing such a harmless question. Overly familiar perhaps, but not so intrusive he could take offense. Kai didn't like Eleazar Dantes very much, but there were no secrets in this particular story.

"She saved my ass on Proxima Twelve." Kai chewed and swallowed another forkful of uninspired fish. "I got myself arrested on suspicion of cheating in a gambling establishment." He made most of his money gambling back then. A dangerous enough vocation even before the Alliance publicly declared war against the invading Enriu, it had become even more so by the time Kai reached Proxima Twelve—a remote, relatively untroubled corner during that first year of fighting, but still a world full of scared and riled citizens. The crowds Kai had a habit of falling in with in those days were among the worst, chosen for their tendency to gamble high. That they also tended to lose without grace was an unfortunate tradeoff of the higher stakes.

Dantes's thick eyebrows rose, the expression crinkling his forehead. "Arrested? An upstanding gentleman like yourself?" A hint of malicious humor sharpened the words, but Kai let it slide with tired practice. He knew which fights were worth picking, and this wasn't one of them. He already knew enough to dislike Eleazar Dantes. He was somehow not surprised when Dantes pressed, "And *were* you cheating?"

"No." Kai propped his elbows on the table and leaned forward with a scowl. "I've never cheated at cards in my life. But I'm good at reading people. The owners of the casino didn't think I should be winning so steadily, even if it was only off the other patrons. They called the authorities before I could clear out."

"And how does Miss Vance fit into this charming scenario?"

"She was freelancing for the Proxima Gambling Commission at the time. I don't know if she took pity on me or if she actually realized I was innocent... And I'll *never* understand how she did it. But she convinced the arresting officers to drop all charges and let me go."

"And you've been working together since?"

"Something like that." Despite the subpar food and Dantes's abrasive company, Kai felt a fond smile softening his combative expression. Of course, it hadn't been nearly so simple. He'd stayed in the neighborhood and kept a curious eye out for the woman who had saved his proverbial bacon. When her post at the Gambling Commission cut short—the Commission all but closing down when the Proxima System shunted funds into military defense—Kai approached Ilsa to propose a partnership.

Convincing her hadn't been easy. The Alliance was fighting for its own existence against an enemy content to destroy what it couldn't claim. One by one, the sectors were falling to chaos, and there was high demand for the tech skills Ilsa could offer. Kai liked to think it had been his earnest charm that sold Ilsa on his proposition, but it was much more likely she simply conceded the advantage of having an ally on rocky terrain.

War was no time to insist on standing alone.

"That must have been quite some time ago." Dantes's gruff voice drew Kai back to the unproductive present.

"Seven years," Kai agreed. It felt like a lifetime, somehow. The only seven years that mattered. He and Ilsa had guarded each other fiercely through four years of escalating conflict. Then, when the war ended and the Enriu scattered, Kai had learned it was just as good to have a partner during peace. He didn't want to consider what his life now would look like without Ilsa at his back.

A knowing edge crept into Dantes's expression when he asked Kai, "And your relationship now?"

Defensiveness stiffened beneath Kai's skin, and he straightened in his seat. "What *about* our relationship now?"

"You seem quite close," Dantes observed. Despite the bland tone, there was no mistaking his more suggestive meaning. "Yet you keep separate quarters."

"We're not a couple, if that's what you're asking." Kai narrowed his eyes.

"But *you*, at least, would happily consider a different arrangement," Dantes noted with all the confidence of a man speaking a blunt truth.

Cold fury whipped through Kai at the presumption, and for once, he made no effort to keep the ice from his eyes. His mouth thinned, and his brow creased as it lowered into a glare. His fists clenched atop the table as he stared Dantes down, daring him to find some way to compound his offense. Kai would put up with a great deal of irritation for the sake of playing nice with an expensive client, but even enlightened self-interest had its limits.

Dantes didn't appear at all flustered by the open display of wrath, but he did quickly cede the field with a wave of one hand. "I apologize for overstepping the bounds of decorum. Please forget I said anything."

They finished their meal in mismatched flavors of silence: Dantes unworried, Kai stubbornly irate. When they parted ways, Kai barely managed to wish the man a cordial goodbye.

He slept poorly that night. He found himself wound too tightly to drift off. Dantes had thrown him off balance, calling him out for something

Kai had been doing his best to keep at a safe and uncomplicated distance. When Kai did manage to sleep, his dreams were all warmth and wondering, mingled with glimpses of Ilsa's most private smile.

He had barely finished dressing the next morning, just returned from the public shower facilities down the hall, when Ilsa barged through his door. She held one of her smaller data screens clutched in her hands, and her hair hung down her back unrestrained. The owlish look about her told Kai she hadn't actually slept the night before, but her posture and movements were full of energy.

"Good. You're up." She glanced around the room despite the fact that it was exactly the same as her own. "Dantes will be here soon. I think I found something."

Kai didn't have a chance to press for details before the door chime sounded, announcing Dantes's arrival. Unlike Ilsa, who had every right to barge in unannounced, Dantes waited until Kai called a welcome through the door.

Blessedly, Dantes came bearing breakfast—an unexciting array of protein bars and something that barely resembled coffee—and Kai accepted his share of the spoils with gratitude. He put their previous night's intrusive conversation from his mind, confident Dantes wouldn't push his luck a second time, and certainly not in front of Ilsa.

Kai considered the limited options for seating three people in the narrow confines of his rented room. There was minimal furniture: a single chair, a poorly balanced table near a grubby window, and the bed he hadn't bothered to tidy upon waking. He grabbed the bedcovers and tugged them haphazardly over the length of the mattress, then seated himself at the foot of the bed with breakfast in hand. The wall was cool at his back, the not-coffee hot and bitter across his tongue. Ilsa sat beside him, her legs kicked out straight so that her boot-clad feet extended past the edge of the mattress. She didn't claim her share of breakfast before she settled in, so Dantes set the remaining foodstuffs on the rickety table as he sat in the uncomfortable chair beside it.

Kai swallowed a generous portion of his drink before turning to Ilsa and prompting, "So. You found something."

Ilsa tapped at the screen, sending text and data scrolling along the slate-gray surface. Kai peered over her shoulder. His eyes were drawn to the movement, the lines of code and tightly packed information, but he could interpret none of what he was seeing. He would have to content himself with waiting for Ilsa to provide an explanation, but at least he could be confident she wouldn't keep them waiting long.

"So," Ilsa echoed. "I've been trawling the private financial networks that pass through this system. And not to be dramatic about it, but... I hit pay dirt." She kept her eyes on the ceaseless scroll of data as she spoke. "The transactions were all buried—*deliberately* buried—about as far down as it's possible to go. Every trick in the book and then some. False receipts, ghost accounts, fraudulent transfers, pre-coded markups, straw men. Not to mention a bunch of ploys I've never even seen before. I've never seen anyone cover their tracks this well."

"And you think these transactions have something to do with Abigail?" Dantes concluded aloud.

"I know they do. They're covered in her digital fingerprints."

From across the room, Dantes looked downright skeptical, and Kai wasn't surprised to hear the man protest, "If she covered her tracks so completely, how can you be sure it's really her?"

Ilsa raised her eyes from the screen and opened her mouth to answer.

"We don't want an explanation," Kai intervened, locking Dantes with a warning look. "Trust me. You and I wouldn't follow a fraction of the groundwork, and the rest won't be any help."

Dantes threw him a dubious glance.

"I mean it. You're better off taking her word for it," Kai promised, holding his ground. The alternative was at least an hour of detailed lecture that Kai had heard more than once and still couldn't follow. Better by far for Dantes to simply let Ilsa cut ahead and give them the broad strokes.

"Besides," Ilsa interrupted their staring contest, leveling a hard look at each of them in turn. "The *how* doesn't matter. The point I'm trying to make here is that these measures were taken to mask an enormous quantity of money."

"How much money?" Kai's brow furrowed faintly.

"I'm honestly not sure," Ilsa admitted. "I don't think I've found it all yet. But I'm reasonably sure I know where most of it was going. These funds are *staggering*. Investments, subsidies, capital being shunted down a hundred tributaries into alternate markets. Which raises some particular questions."

"What was she doing with that kind of money?" Kai finished connecting the dots laid out before him. "And where did it come from in the first place?"

"Exactly." Ilsa nodded approval. "Unfortunately, it could take days to find more complete answers. I'll have to dig deeper, try and retrace our steps to make sure I didn't miss something along the way—"

"You'll have to do no such thing," Dantes interjected. Kai and Ilsa both stared at him, but he looked entirely unconcerned as he explained, "I know perfectly well where the money came from. I gave it to her."

In his peripheral vision, Kai saw Ilsa go perfectly, furiously still. The text on her data screen stopped scrolling, and her spine and shoulders tightened. Kai felt matching frustration bloom in his own chest, and it was through gritted teeth that he made himself speak.

"Why the *fuck* are you only telling us this information now?"

To his limited credit, Dantes looked genuinely perplexed. "I didn't think it was relevant. Why are you angry with me?"

"Because we could have been tracking the *money* this entire time!" Ilsa's knuckles were white where she gripped the hard edges of her data screen, and her voice was more snarl than speech. "The traces I've found on this network? They're not the beginning of the trail, and they're certainly not the *end* of the trail. If I'd known there were sizable financial records to follow, we could have saved ourselves *days* of unnecessary work. Money is a hundred times easier to track than an individual human."

The force of her ire gave Dantes visible pause, or maybe it was the import of her words hitting him. He'd already demonstrated how anxious he was to find his daughter; the thought of wasting unnecessary time *should* trouble him. Kai did his best to swallow back the worst of his own anger. He set a hand on Ilsa's shoulder in what he hoped was a calming gesture, wordlessly urging her to ease back.

"I apologize." Dantes sounded genuinely regretful. "I didn't intend to waste your efforts or your time."

Ilsa huffed, but the tension bled from her posture with the low exhale. "It's fine." She sounded conciliatory, if not necessarily forgiving. "Just... no more leaving details out, okay? *We'll* decide what information is relevant."

"Of course," Dantes agreed, and then pressed, "Where does that leave us? What comes next?"

"Next we get off this rock." Ilsa returned to her screen, tapping the corner to pull up a different wall of information. Her eyes skimmed back and forth, weighing possibilities, gauging the path ahead. "Most of these transactions are pointing the same direction, and I can dig a little deeper once we're on the road. Patching into local networks will help."

"Where to first?" Kai asked.

"Ravelle, I think," Ilsa murmured. She already sounded distracted, and Kai recognized the matrix of transport manifests that had expanded to cover the bulk of her screen. "There are no direct transports, but I can book us on an outbound courier that departs from Chasper tomorrow. It's heading the right direction, more or less."

"Excellent." Kai would be glad to put Chasper's dire facilities behind him, and 'more or less' was good enough for a start.

CHAPTER FOUR

They stayed steadily on the move once they put Chasper and the T'i Yara system behind them, pausing only long enough for Ilsa to unearth more of Abigail's trail of financial breadcrumbs. Three separate stops were necessary before reaching Ravelle. All three layovers were small ports, with few travelers and even fewer tourists, but at every stop Ilsa was able to dig deeper. She did what she could on the road, but most ships—*all* the ships on which they managed to arrange short-notice accommodations—offered only limited communication linkups. The crew could access more reliable tools, but passengers weren't afforded the same resources, and Ilsa preferred not to patch in illegally.

The limitations posed no great difficulty. She found ample information during their brief layovers, and slowly she began to untangle a web even more complex than she'd first predicted.

They stayed constantly on the move, spending only a night or two in each port, even less time if there was transport available and Ilsa could complete her work more quickly.

She preferred to be on the move. The vessels they found on short notice offered berths even smaller than those available on the most crowded stations, but Ilsa still preferred them to the alternative. She found a ship in transit less claustrophobic simply because she was bound *somewhere*, not sitting stationary in space. Contradictory reasoning, perhaps, but the knowledge that they were moving helped her settle just the same.

On arriving at Ravelle, Kai drew her aside and said, "Someone is following us."

Ilsa's insides chilled. It certainly wouldn't be the first time they'd dealt with someone dogging their steps, but instinct told her this situation was different. Last time it had been a second investigator hired by their own client, a suspicious and mistrustful Vrean with more money than sense. Surely that couldn't be the case now. Not with Eleazar Dantes himself along for the ride on his own insistence.

"Are you sure?" The question felt foolish on her tongue. Of course Kai was sure. "Who?" Ilsa amended before he could answer.

"A small Gaiminn. Kri, I think." That last meant little to Ilsa. She couldn't have described the relevant features, let alone told at a glance which continent or planet a particular Gaiminn was from. But she could conjure a general image clearly enough, of faintly iridescent hide and two parallel pairs of eyes, a thin mouth tucked so near the chin it would be easy to miss entirely. Patchy hair, or something like it—Ilsa wasn't sure; she had never been a student of biology.

"How long have they been following us?" she asked quietly.

"I first saw her on the frigate we caught out of Magre. There were at least a dozen commercial passengers on that flight. I didn't pay any real mind until I saw her at both our last two stops."

"It could still be coincidence," Ilsa said, both unconvincing and unconvinced. "Is she here now?"

Ravelle was an enormous port, built like scrawling script across the only desert plateau of an otherwise hospitable planet. It was the largest of three different docking facilities positioned across the planet's surface, and partner to a twin base on the moon orbiting immediately overhead. If coincidence were a viable explanation, there was no reason their paths should cross here.

"I saw her on the lower concourse," Kai said, blowing the faint hope away like so much debris.

"We need to tell Dantes." Ilsa glanced behind her now, toward the customs gate she and Kai had just emerged through. She could see Dantes at one of the nearer kiosks, impatiently concluding his business with a bored customs official.

"Yes," Kai agreed. "And we need to stay alert. I can't be sure our tail is alone. My gut says she brought backup."

They remained at Ravelle only a day and a half, cutting short Ilsa's efforts to unearth the data she needed. They departed early, and as discreetly as they could manage. From there they hopped in quick succession between smaller way stations along the Allis Belt. Ilsa focused on her own work and trusted Kai to watch for danger.

"She's not alone," he announced to Ilsa and Dantes both when they arrived at the eerily quiet Depsis dock—a nearly defunct facility beside a failing mining operation. "And whoever she's traveling with, I think there are more of them now. I don't like it, especially not here."

"You think they intend to try something?" Dantes's eyes darted about the silent corridor, though of course, there was nothing to see. No one in sight. There was an unnatural stillness to the empty hall, and Ilsa didn't like it one bit.

"You don't call that many hands on deck unless you're looking for a fight," Kai answered dully. Ilsa was already fishing in her rucksack for the firearm she carried. The weapon was a small, subtle affair, but it packed a heavy wallop. It wouldn't punch through bulkheads even on its highest setting; the design was meant to be wielded both within an atmosphere and in less terrestrial locales. The charge could be set low enough that it *might* not kill, but the discharge—energy crammed into bullet-sized blasts that could tear through flesh at higher settings—might still cause heart failure in most Alliance species.

"Where did you see them?" She checked the power reserves on her gun. The weapon was fully charged. She'd been doubly careful since Kai first caught sight of their suspicious shadow.

"They disembarked a ways behind us, but I lost sight before the arrivals gate."

Ilsa cursed under her breath. The arrivals gate had been a veritable dead zone, a dozen passengers threading narrow halls away from the main docks. If the Gaiminn and her friends had disappeared so abruptly, they must have an alternate way past the security crews. They could be anywhere by now. Chances were damn high that they were close.

She glanced to her left and saw Dantes had drawn a gun from somewhere as well. Dantes's weapon was larger, nothing subtle about it, bulky and gray. The metal was so clean Ilsa would swear it had never been fired. She recognized the make only vaguely, and had never seen the model before. If she had to guess, based solely on its size and the fact that Dantes was the one carrying it, she'd say the gun was both flashy and overkill. She doubted the thing even had a low-power setting.

"We can't avoid them if we don't know where they *are*," Ilsa hissed, glancing between her companions and doing her best to keep a cool head. She tried to think her way past the trap she could suddenly sense closing in around them, but it was difficult to strategize with so little information at hand.

"Maybe we can—" Kai began, but cut himself off when the corridor went abruptly dark.

Ilsa clenched her teeth to keep down the startled curse that threatened to crawl up her throat. To her left, Dantes went perfectly still. To her right, Kai was already turning, eyes darting forward along the darkened hall.

The blackness wasn't pitch. There were occasional panels of faint light, the glow of power conduits glinting behind the walls at nearly regular intervals. There were also windows—tiny, narrow things tucked near the ceiling—offering scant illumination from outside. It was night on this side of the planet, but two moons shared the sky, and the ambient light was better than having none at all. Ilsa shrugged her rucksack off her shoulders, maneuvering in complete silence as she set it on the floor. It tucked almost invisible into a shallow inset in a corner of one wall, and Ilsa cocked her head, wordlessly urging Kai to do the same with his bag. She crept forward while he obeyed. Her eyes gradually adjusted to the gloom, and she peered down the hall, to where the corridor narrowed and turned.

By the time Ilsa risked shifting her attention behind her, Dantes's travel case was also out of sight, as well as Kai's worn jacket.

Kai was rolling up his shirtsleeves and watching Ilsa with sharp focus.

"What do we do?" Dantes asked, his voice pitched so low Ilsa strained to hear him.

"*You* stay here," Kai ordered, soft steel in his voice as he turned to look Dantes directly in the eye. "Ilsa and I will move up the corridor and see what's ahead."

Ilsa wanted to order Kai to stay back and keep *his* head down too, but she could already see Dantes rankling, ruffling himself up to protest. The last thing Kai needed was Ilsa arguing tactics in front of their contentious employer; they needed to present a unified front if they were going to keep Dantes from throwing himself into the line of fire. He was a client, an uninvited tagalong and a liability—and he had no place at their backs if they were walking into something messy.

So instead of countering Kai's assertion, Ilsa leveled a steady stare at Dantes in turn. "Seriously. *Stay put.* We need to check this out, and we don't have time to teach you our shorthand. We'll hurry back."

Reluctantly—angrily—Dantes subsided. Kai nodded, then turned to follow Ilsa straight ahead. Whether he let her take the lead as thanks for backing his play, or simply because he himself was maneuvering empty-handed, Ilsa didn't know or care.

She moved as silently as she could, reaching the corner at the narrow end of the hall and crouching low to peer around it.

There was only another empty hallway ahead, but she still straightened and inched forward with all possible caution.

"You lied to him," Kai murmured in her ear, keeping close but also moving with measured vigilance.

"About what?"

"We haven't rehearsed any shorthand." There was laughter in Kai's voice, despite the fact that his words were barely audible—despite the danger and severity of the situation—and Ilsa found herself smiling.

"Near enough. Anyway, our standard contract has a clause that covers lying to clients for their own good." She wanted to say more, maybe tell him to be *careful,* goddamn it, but they were halfway through the smaller corridor now, and there was an open hatch directly ahead. It was a large door, wide and tall, and from the handful of crate-shaped silhouettes cluttered in front of it, Ilsa guessed it was the sigma-side loading bay they needed to cross to reach the main complex. She fell quiet, keeping her footfalls soft as she passed the first of the skinny crates.

Ilsa stopped when she reached the door. She plastered herself to the frame and waited as Kai mirrored her position on the opposite side. Again she crouched, her heart hammering so noisily in her chest that it was a shock the entire port couldn't hear her. She felt lightheaded, but her hands were steady as she peered with one eye into the space beyond the door.

Inside her head echoed a wild mantra of curses, a violent mix of anger and fear. She and Kai weren't prepared for this. They weren't *trained* for this. They'd come out all right from situations that smelled just as awful, but luck and perfect aim couldn't carry them forever.

Luck and perfect aim were all they had going for them, though. Ilsa could see no one in the dim expanse of the room beyond the open doorframe. It was a fraction brighter than the corridor, a space with windows spanning most of one wall and a skylight at the farthest end. There was still no artificial light—whoever had deactivated the system had clearly done it for this entire section of the docking grid—but the two moons were visible and their combined glow slanted across the floor.

As she'd suspected, the room itself was a long loading bay. The wall opposite the windows looked to be one enormous apparatus that must open to accommodate ramps from heavily stocked ships. Huge cargo containers stood throughout the vast space, looking indistinguishable from each other in the gray darkness. Rectangular blobs of shadow. At least they could provide solid cover, Ilsa thought, for whatever that might prove worth.

The ceiling stretched at least two stories high, and catwalks ran above the two walls Ilsa could see from her limited vantage. She had to assume those paths extended directly above the doorframe. If there were armed enemies waiting up there, they would be directly above and out of sight. Ilsa could see nobody at all from her current position.

She subsided, drawing back from the frame and watching Kai do the same opposite her. He met her eyes through the murky gloom. As he rose from crouching, he had the distinct look of a trap ready to spring.

Ilsa rose too, checking her gun. She considered only briefly before tapping in the sequence that would set every shot she fired to lethal force. She had no qualms about killing those who meant her harm, and no doubt at all that whoever was waiting to ambush them meant to kill without remorse.

She met Kai's eyes with determination and gestured with her free hand, indicating the mechanical wall opposite the windows. It wasn't a rehearsed signal. It meant nothing more complicated than *that way, go fast,* just in case he hadn't seen the catwalk and its looming promise of hidden attackers.

Kai nodded his understanding, and they waited. Breathed in unison, out and then in. Perfect silence. Perfect stillness. Perfect understanding passing between them. Then, in a single instant, they came to life and charged forward.

They moved together through the door and darted for cover near the shadowed wall.

Gunfire erupted around them, staccato bursts of heat and light blasting through the air. Surprise was a fleeting advantage, but it kept Ilsa and Kai one step ahead of the barrage as they barreled across open ground. It felt like an eternity before they finally reached cover behind the smooth metal of an enormous cargo crate. Ilsa hit the ground harder than she intended, and her knees protested the impact. She was already moving again, craning around the far side of the crate.

She spotted two figures scrambling across the catwalk, exactly where she'd expected. They were rushing now toward the nearest flimsy ladder. For the moment they were entirely exposed, and Ilsa took careful aim before the flicker of opportunity passed.

She breathed through the roar of adrenaline in her ears, steadied her weapon with both hands, and fired.

The figure in the lead went down, choked shout carrying loudly through the vast bay. The body didn't slip from the catwalk but instead crumpled directly forward onto the narrow metal path.

The second figure stumbled over the fallen shadow. Ilsa's next shot landed just as surely as the first, and the second shadow fell.

There was shouting then, close by, in at least two languages—Gaime and something Ilsa didn't recognize—and then sparks ignited against the crate just above her head. Those shots sliced *through* the corner of the crate where there wasn't enough mass to deflect the energy, and Ilsa cursed aloud just as gravity seemed to yank her out of harm's way.

Except it wasn't gravity saving her. It was Kai, his hands clutching her arms with bruising force, his bulk landing beneath her as she fell. They both scrambled upright and pressed flat against smooth metal as gunfire thudded, noisy and ugly, against the far side of the crate. Head-on, the container was large enough to absorb the impacts and burning charges, but it wouldn't hold forever. And it wouldn't protect them when the enemy finally circled around and flanked them.

"There are only three more of them out there." Kai's words were a cautious hiss in Ilsa's ear.

"You're sure?" she whispered back.

Kai nodded.

"Can you get to them?" She glanced downward and fussed by feel with the settings of her weapon. Wider bursts would require more energy—she would drain her weapon faster, would have only a few minutes of power left—but a wider range would also distract and blind, at least momentarily. Kai would never get close enough if she didn't draw and keep the enemy's attention.

"I think so," Kai said. Then he spoke her name in a tone she'd never heard before. He sounded almost hesitant, and confusion caught at Ilsa's insides as she raised her gaze.

She could barely see him now beyond his silhouette and the reflective glint of his eyes. She could make out no hint of his expression, and the tension in his shoulders told her nothing, considering they were actively under attack.

"Kai?"

He moved forward all at once, a surge of shadows closing the slim distance that separated them. He paid no heed at all to the weapon in Ilsa's hand as he cupped the back of her head in one huge palm and pressed a hard kiss to her mouth. The kiss was hurried and desperate, and over in an uncomfortable instant. Ilsa didn't even try to process what had just happened. Kai was already creeping toward the far corner of the crate, and she needed to be ready to make the first move.

"Let me get into position," she hissed over her shoulder, watched for the quick nod of assent that told her he'd heard the instruction. Then she threw herself into the open, running with all the speed her legs could summon.

She covered twenty paces in a protracted instant, viscerally aware of the singeing cannonade of weapons fire close on her heels. She ducked and rolled low as she reached the next piece of cover. Not one large crate this time, but a sturdy stack of smaller containers. These were dull, dark metal, piled deeply enough that even the most powerful volley lost its momentum before it could burst through to Ilsa's protected position.

She gave herself no time to cower, or to think, or even to breathe. She ducked for the far side of her new hiding place and fired, angling for the corner from which most of the attacks had come. She wasn't bothering to aim, though she tried to give the illusion of it as she discharged her weapon.

She fired. Paused. Let the worst of the returning gunfire fade. Twisted and fired again. She had to keep them focused on her until—

Yes, there was noticeably less speed to the answering bombardment a moment later. Ilsa tilted her own aim farther off target—the last thing she wanted to do was catch Kai in an unlucky shot—and slowed her finger on the trigger of her gun.

When she stopped shooting and was met with only silence, she tentatively peered around the edge of her hiding place. The stack of crates wobbled beneath her hand—not so sturdy after the prolonged assault—but Ilsa could see nothing in the darkened bay. Nothing in the shadows, nothing on the catwalks.

Nothing until Kai warily appeared in a patch of moonlight. He stood upright, glancing stiffly around himself as he crossed the open space. For all his caution, Ilsa realized he had already backtracked and double checked his work. Kai must have been sure he'd gotten everyone, or he wouldn't be moving out in the open. Ilsa glimpsed no bodies in the heavy darkness. The only dead she could see were her first two victims, the barely visible forms on the catwalk above the door.

Kai was holding his shoulder too tightly, and as Ilsa emerged into moonlight she saw why.

"God*damn* it, Kai."

He was bleeding. His dark shirt might not show it, but his pale skin certainly did where the fabric was torn beneath his hand. When she got close enough to set her gun down and draw his hand away from the wound, his palm was soaked. The red of his blood looked black in the moonlight.

"It's not that bad," Kai protested, but Ilsa only glared at him.

"It's bad enough." She tried to be gentle as she prodded at his shoulder around the wound, but Kai still flinched and bit his lower lip. Ilsa's medical training was little more than basic wartime first aid, but it told her this was a deeper wound than Kai was admitting. It wasn't singed around the edges or cauterized the way gunfire from those weapons should have been, which meant one of Kai's hand-to-hand opponents must have drawn a knife on him. Ilsa scowled. Her rucksack had bandages tucked in one of the side pockets, but Kai would need an actual physician. She certainly wasn't skilled enough to stitch him up herself.

"Come on. Bandages." She finally stepped back, picked up her gun, and moved for the door that had brought them. Kai immediately covered the gash with his hand as he followed her, pressing hard despite the amount of discomfort his efforts clearly caused him. Struggling to staunch the bleeding.

They needed to collect Dantes, but he was barely a footnote to Ilsa's awareness at the moment. Dantes would still be in the previous corridor, in the general proximity of Ilsa's limited first aid supplies. That was good enough for the time being.

"*This* is why you need a fucking gun," Ilsa muttered, moving quickly but still with wary caution through the dark hall.

"Can we not have this argument right now?" Kai was audibly winded, but otherwise his low voice gave no hint that he was hurt. If anything, he sounded exasperated, and well he might. They'd certainly disagreed on this point often enough in seven years of partnership, and Ilsa had yet to win the debate.

"Now seems like the perfect time to me," she retorted, more to settle her own nerves than because she really thought this was the time or the place to harp on Kai's stubbornness. Over half the length of their partnership had been dedicated to surviving a war. If she couldn't convince him to carry a proper weapon then, she had no hope of managing the trick now.

"I don't like guns. I've got terrible aim."

"Aim improves with practice." Ilsa stopped and glanced about herself. They'd already rounded the narrow corner into the wider stretch of corridor, and she'd been sure this was where they had parted from Dantes. Was it possible they'd taken a wrong turn? It seemed unlikely in such a short distance, and she didn't remember any unexpected doorways or passages.

When she glanced downward, she found her rucksack wedged right where she'd left it. This *was* the place.

Adrenaline rushed beneath her skin in a renewed surge, but she crouched beside the bag and unfastened the side flap. She had to dig beneath a supply of ration bars and a hand light to reach the small first-aid pack, and she nearly fumbled the entire lot as she tore open a clean bandage.

They didn't have time to properly clean or disinfect the wound. If Dantes wasn't here, then there could still be hostiles to contend with. Ilsa rose to find Kai had already let go of his shoulder and torn his demolished sleeve open wider to give her space to work. The bandage affixed easily, sealing to the intact skin around the wound despite the slick and drying mess of blood already spilled. It would have to do for the moment.

Crouching again, Ilsa picked up the hand light she'd dropped in her haste to reach the bandages. She hesitated a moment, not yet activating it, and glanced down the long corridor to take stock in the dimness. The hall branched in several directions at the far end, including downward. Ilsa saw no movement, no sign of life at all, and when she glanced to Kai for confirmation, he shook his head. He could see no threat either.

The hand light was a small, focused thing, and it gave off almost no ambient glare when she turned it on. It lit only a square patch of ground directly where she aimed it. Ilsa swept the floor quickly but methodically, not entirely sure what she was looking for.

She stopped when she found it. Dantes's gun lay abandoned not far from where Ilsa remembered leaving him. It was equipped and active, and the barrel was warm to the touch. He must have been shooting when he dropped it. If it weren't for the deafening assault of more immediate gunfire, Kai and Ilsa would have heard the sounds of combat.

There was blood two feet from the fallen weapon, slicked across the hard ground.

"Red," Ilsa reported. There was enough of it to make the puddle impossible to mistake, but not enough to indicate a mortal wound. She hoped not, anyway. It was difficult to be sure.

"Probably his." Kai stood a short distance from her, peering at the walls despite the dimness of the hall. "I didn't see any humans in the posse on our tail." He paused, peered closer at a stretch of wall that looked not at all special at a distance, and then announced in the same low voice, "There are half a dozen scorch marks here, and at least one shot went clean through the wall. Looks like Dantes went down fighting."

"Of course he did." Ilsa tried to picture the man meekly surrendering, even for his own good, and couldn't conjure a convincing image. "I suppose we'd better find him and make sure he's alive."

"And rescue him," Kai agreed. He sounded lighthearted enough, but there was steel tucked beneath the words. Ilsa picked up her own weapon, secured and deactivated it, and slipped it into the pocket of her long coat. She kept the coat on—it was dark and discreet, and she didn't need the same maneuverability Kai required—not wanting to leave her weapon behind despite the fact that it was running fatally low on power. She'd rather have those two or three remaining shots at her disposal.

Before she stood, she took Dantes's gun in hand, gauging the balance in her grip. It was a bulky weapon, heavier than it looked, but she had practiced on bigger monstrosities. She felt confident her aim would hold true.

"Here." Ilsa handed her light to Kai. She would need both hands to manage Dantes's gun. "We'll need it to follow his trail." Assuming he'd left them one.

He *had* left a trail. The infrequent patches of blood became scanter with every turn and corridor, but they were enough to guide Kai and Ilsa along a steady course. Dantes was still bleeding as his captors directed him... Where? Ilsa wasn't familiar enough with Depsis to know where they were going without the advantage of a map, and they were well beyond the commercial portions of the facility. There were no directional kiosks here. And they were only moving deeper, into dull-sided corridors where doors were labeled only with strings of numbers. They were underground, Ilsa realized. They had descended more than one flight of stairs along the way, and the air had cooled. There were no more windows offering illumination from outside.

There was other light now, though. Not just safety lights, but the occasional overhead panel set to a default night setting. This wasn't the deliberate gloom of sabotaged hallways. These were simply corridors disused at so late an hour, minimal lighting designed to save power. It was enough for Kai to put the hand light away, and Ilsa immediately felt less exposed.

She caught sight of a brighter glare ahead before she heard any voices, but in a few more paces, she could make out words—Terran standard—in angry conversation.

"—the hell are you doing with that thing?" Dantes's unmistakable voice cut through the quiet with surprising calm. "Is that a recording device? Can't we just get this over with, clean and quick?"

Ilsa and Kai exchanged a look, eyebrows high. They had reached the source of the light, an open door frame halfway down the empty hall. Ilsa reached the door first and crouched beside it, Dantes's gun held steady in both hands. She leaned just far enough to get a look inside, praying their quarry was overconfident enough to not be watching the door too closely.

There were only three figures in the room besides Dantes, and none of them seemed to notice her. Two were feathered fellows, round and disconcertingly pillow-like. They wore matching gray bodysuits that looked uncomfortable over their dark feathers, and each held a shock rifle in hand as they stood at stiff attention. They loomed behind Dantes, where he knelt with wrists bound before him.

Posed for execution.

The third figure was almost certainly the Gaiminn tracker Kai had first spotted. She *was* shorter than average, her skin loose and sleek and faintly purple. She stood directly in front of Dantes, fussing with a small piece of equipment that hovered on a blurry sheen of air. Ilsa didn't need a good look to be sure Dantes was right. That was some sort of recording-and-transmission device.

"Cease talking," the Gaiminn snapped. At last she stepped away from the tripod, clearly finished with her work.

Dantes surprised no one—clearly not even his captors—by continuing to speak. "Bad enough you intend to blow my brains across the floor. Do you really need to document the event for posterity?"

The Gaiminn made a clucking noise with her tongue. It sounded eerily like laughter. "Sir Iain Merck insists on proof the job is done. Therefore proof he shall be given. *You* do not have any say in the matter."

"Iain Merck, eh?" Dantes sounded unimpressed. "And here I'd hoped you were working for someone with a legitimate grudge."

Whatever else Ilsa might have hoped to glean from the conversation, she realized her time was running out. The Gaiminn moved to a greater distance, presumably out of range to let her feathered companions work, and the two toughs were beginning to raise their weapons. Ilsa hefted Dantes's gun. She sent a quick, silent prayer to gods she'd never bothered to believe in, and then pulled the trigger.

She dropped the first tough more by luck than skill. Dantes's gun erred to the left, and she was damn lucky to still catch her target high in the chest. A weaker gun or lower setting might have left her target alive from such a glancing blow, but the residual charge packed too much kick. The figure fell hard, convulsing just long enough to give the appearance of pain before falling permanently still.

The second tough squawked in startled protest. He whirled for the door, searching her out, but Ilsa dropped him too, efficiently and without remorse. Unlike the first, her second shot landed with cold accuracy.

She searched, discovered the Gaiminn had retreated to the far side of the room and was now struggling with a locked door. It was more practicality than pity that made Ilsa aim for the wall beside instead of the Gaiminn's head, a warning shot across the enemy bough. If they took the ringleader alive, perhaps they could get further answers. At minimum they'd have someone to turn over to the authorities rather than having to hit the road in order to avoid an ugly cleanup.

But the Gaiminn didn't surrender at the violent warning. Instead she dropped to one knee and pivoted, drawing a compact weapon from beneath her vest.

Ilsa recognized the gun as a Mirror Line 56G—a model Ilsa was partial to herself—before she had to duck behind the doorframe to avoid the shot that scorched past her face. Ilsa swung forward once more, leading with Dantes's weapon and exhaling as she moved, taking quick, deadly aim. She pulled the trigger and the Gaiminn fell, leaving the room empty but for Dantes himself and the guilty dead.

It was Kai who darted into the room to cut Dantes loose, leaving Ilsa to destroy the recording device before it could catch their faces. They vacated the premises in a hurry, retracing their steps in grim silence. As far as Ilsa could tell, Dantes wasn't bleeding anymore. At the very least he was well enough to keep his mouth shut, and that suited her fine for the moment.

It wasn't until they'd recovered their belongings and reached a more populous district that Kai turned to Dantes and asked, "Who is Sir Iain Merck?" Kai's voice was strained and tired. With his coat on, there was no visible sign of his injury, but Ilsa knew he was beginning to bleed through the bandage. She carried both her own bag and Kai's, despite Kai's attempt to insist otherwise. He looked too pale, unsteady on his feet, and Ilsa refused to let him push his luck. She barely listened now as Kai questioned Dantes. She was too busy looking for an open clinic as they moved from dockside to more of a market plaza, where merchants were just beginning to prepare for the morning.

"Iain Merck was a competitor of mine," Dantes answered without apparent evasion. "He exercised many of the same leveraging tactics as I did during the war, but he did it on my turf. He lacked the capital to back up his maneuvering. When I drove him out of the system, I absorbed all his holdings. I suppose he harbors some bad feelings."

Kai laughed, a strained sound that was more dry than amused. "And this you *don't* call a legitimate grudge?"

In her peripheral vision, Ilsa saw Dantes shrug. "I don't make kind choices, Mr. Othen. A successful man accumulates enemies."

Ilsa snorted, but didn't comment beyond asserting, "We'll need to book a flight straight out of here once we find someone to mend Kai. There's too much chance authorities will connect us to the mess if we stay."

"What about the local data stream?" Kai asked, speeding his steps to walk beside her.

"I'll manage with the next one. It's not a static trail we're following. I know what I'm looking for now. It's no disaster if I don't get access to one link in the chain." It could make her work more difficult, but only for a short while. She'd rather have to manage digital gymnastics to fill in some blanks than get them all arrested by insisting they stay.

"There." Kai pointed to a pale blue sign bearing an empty circle—the universal symbol for Alliance-licensed medical care. The door beside the sign was shut; the doctor clearly wasn't open for business yet. Ilsa altered course anyway, making straight for that door.

She didn't care what time of day it was. She would raise a ruckus until someone answered, and then she would pay whatever tender was required. She had no intention of watching Kai bleed to death.

"Relax," Kai murmured for Ilsa's ears only. "I'll be fine."

"You goddamn better be." Ilsa pounded on the door.

CHAPTER FIVE

Largest of Lannis's habitable moons, Lanniah Ceti Three boasted the busiest port in the solar system. It was also far enough from Depsis that Kai felt better for the distance, even if his mended shoulder ached and itched every moment of the journey. Ilsa reminded him more than once that the discomfort was entirely in his head; the medic had done a professional job patching the deep wound, not just with needle and thread but with respectable technologies to speed the body's natural repair processes.

Kai didn't care. It itched. And it wouldn't *stop* itching until he could take the damn bandage off and put the entire ordeal behind him. It didn't help that Dantes seemed to consider it perfectly reasonable that Kai should have been injured in his service. Dantes seemed to take the fight and rescue for granted, never once thanking them for hauling his ungrateful ass out of harm's way. Kai rankled at the presumption. If Dantes had remained behind from the start and simply allowed Kai and Ilsa to follow their usual procedure, working alone and reporting progress from a distance, they could have avoided the situation entirely. There would've been no attack in the first place if Kai and Ilsa had been traveling alone.

He silently conceded that there was no point confronting a man like Eleazar Dantes about ingratitude, and he swallowed his irritation silently. Ilsa seemed to be doing the same. They would have to make do with Dantes's reassurances of traveling beyond Iain Merck's sphere of influence.

They arrived at port during the midday rush and exited their small passenger frigate into regulated chaos. There were large crowds disembarking, a dozen other vessels standing parked in an orderly row along the airfield. The port facilities were a short distance away, a building so wide it looked squat despite stretching nine stories tall.

Sections of the ground were marked off, designating moving walkways, and elsewhere there were hovering carts offering rides toward the main building. The walkways were overcrowded, and the carts demanded payment for services—up front, no free rides—but Kai and Ilsa didn't mind the longer walk. Ilsa especially seemed in no hurry to leave the open air, crisp and cool with a vividly clear sky overhead.

More surprising was Dantes following meekly without complaint, and without requisitioning one of those passing carts. Perhaps he felt guilty for endangering them after all. It was the only explanation Kai could muster for the silent concession.

Two days later, Kai was bandage-free. The unmarred skin of his shoulder gave no indication that he had almost bled to death on Depsis. Kai recognized his near miss more from the frantic fear in Ilsa's eyes than from his own lightheaded memories of pain, but at least he felt at home in his own skin once more.

He also felt restless, as two days had passed without any useful task on which to spend his focus. Their search was no longer following Abigail's physical trail. The pressure was now entirely on Ilsa as she narrowed in closer on the traces of capital Abigail had been so keen to hide. Kai doubted Abigail had physically set foot in most of the ports they were passing through now, but it didn't matter if she had. The trail they were on was all investments and business portfolios. Dantes was of some use when Ilsa had questions about the meaning of what she was finding, but this was all far beyond Kai's purview and even farther beyond his skills. It wasn't the first time he'd landed on this side of a labor disparity in their usually efficient partnership, but it was the first time the lack of utility had thrown him quite so hard off his stride.

In the absence of ways to make himself useful, Kai had too much time to think. Ilsa was never far from his mind—she was his partner and his closest friend—but after the loading bay on Depsis, he found her distracting in ways he usually managed to avoid.

He didn't want to admit he might be in love with his partner. Love was complicated and difficult, and in Kai's limited experience, it tended to end badly. But he had kissed Ilsa. A fleeting, ill-timed kiss that taunted his memory and left him wanting more. There was no point pretending he didn't want to do it her again, properly this time.

In two days of inaction, the wanting had only gotten worse.

Their third day on Lanniah Ceti Three, Kai acknowledged the truth with painful clarity.

There was no uncertainty left in this equation. He was in love with Ilsa Vance.

And partner or not, he couldn't keep the revelation quietly to himself.

Ilsa's room was in the same hall as Kai's, on the seventh floor of a massive building that did double duty as a hostel and dockside business nexus. The upper levels were all rooms for rent, and Dantes had booked himself a larger suite on the nineteenth floor despite the fact that the smaller rooms on the seventh were perfectly pleasant and well equipped. Kai hadn't made any effort to talk Dantes out of his course. It was a relief to have their intrusive client a little farther out of reach. Dantes still managed to make a nuisance of himself, turning up, checking in, pinging them over the building's personal communications network. But he wasn't right next door, and in this moment especially, Kai was grateful for the reprieve.

In the narrow hallway, he had only one corner to turn before he reached Ilsa's room. For the first time in years, he hesitated. Neither of them had any qualms about barging through the other's door unannounced, but this was different.

This wasn't business as usual. This was a conversation apt to change all the rules.

Kai pressed the panel beside the door.

He could just barely hear the low-pitched tone announcing his presence, and a moment later the door slid open. Ilsa stood on the other side, a look of forced patience on her face. She was clearly expecting Dantes. When she caught sight of Kai, her expression changed to mild confusion.

She stood back and gestured him inside. Kai took a step across the threshold, painfully aware of the nervous tension simmering beneath his skin. The door slid automatically closed behind him, leaving him beside Ilsa in a spacious single room with wide windows. Ilsa had raised the transparent panes despite the intense afternoon heat, and the room's climate adjusters were audibly struggling to compensate for the inhospitable open air.

"Everything okay?" Ilsa asked. There was uncharacteristic wariness in her voice, and Kai felt a twinge of guilt for putting it there.

He suddenly wished he had rehearsed this before storming his way to her door. Ilsa's question demanded a better answer than the disingenuous, "Fine," that was all he managed to muster up. He looked at her with new awareness, wondering how he'd ever been able to pretend his feelings away. Her face was gorgeous, the rest of her just as distracting. Ilsa favored comfortable clothing, fabrics that didn't cling too tightly or restrict her movements, but there was no mistaking the pleasant contours of her figure. She was dressed now in a shirt with a low neckline and barely any sleeves, concession to the dry heat of their current layover. Her hair was wet from a recent shower, and damp curls clung to her neck and draped between her shoulder blades.

Ilsa took a cautious step toward him, dark eyes searching his face. "You don't look fine." She eyed him warily. "You look like you've seen something frightful. What's wrong?"

Kai had to bite his lower lip to prevent a bark of laughter. Ridiculous that realizing he was in love should feel so much like terror. The sliver of mirth vanished almost as quickly as it arose, and Kai drew a slow breath that did nothing at all to steady him.

Ilsa stood directly before him now, paying no heed to Kai's personal space. Their difference in height was even more pronounced at such close range, and she had to tilt her head back to peer sharply into his eyes. She set a hand to his arm and spoke his name with a low edge of fear.

Kai's breath stilled as a feeling like panic swelled in his chest. He had no voice, and even if he had, how could anyone hear it over the racket his pulse was making in his ears? Ilsa was still watching him closely, and Kai moved on instinct, raised a hand to cup her cheek. Ilsa's lips parted, perhaps on a question, and Kai leaned down and in.

She retreated before he could kiss her. A single backward step took her out of range, and her hand disappeared from his arm. Kai blinked in surprised disappointment and, after an awkward moment, let his hand drop to his side.

Ilsa was staring at him now not with worry or fear, but with wide-open shock. "What the fuck are you doing?"

She hadn't retreated any farther than that single step, but Kai possessed enough good sense not to follow. The frantic pounding of his heartbeat took on a different timbre as he realized this wasn't going to go anything like he'd hoped. Ilsa should be in his arms right now, not gawping at him like he'd lost his mind.

"I just thought, now that we're not surrounded by gunfire we might..." He trailed off and an unwilling blush rose to his cheeks.

For several seconds Ilsa regarded him in indecipherable silence.

"I don't understand," she said finally, in a voice gone impossibly quiet. "You're not— If this is about Depsis and that kiss... I figured it was just the heat of the moment."

"It really wasn't." Kai's confession matched Ilsa's sudden quiet. He was watching her intently, and it troubled him that he couldn't tell what she was thinking. Her face was far from blank, but her expression still gave nothing away. She peered up at him for almost a full minute, wordless, her mouth pressed into a thin line.

Fraught impatience tugged beneath his skin, but Kai held himself perfectly still.

Disappointment squeezed his heart when Ilsa turned and made for her desk. She said only, "We have a job to do."

"*Ilsa*," Kai protested, taking a single step in pursuit before his feet froze uselessly to the floor.

"I can't talk about this right now." Ilsa still wasn't looking at him as she dropped into her chair. Her gaze focused determinedly on the haphazard arrangement of screens atop her desk. "I've almost cracked through the final layers of data protection. I need to focus."

It was a curt dismissal, and it stung. Even consoling himself that he'd caught her off guard—that of course she would need time to consider what he was offering—didn't ease the sense of rejection. She was *right*. They had a job to do. But his heart and pride both smarted at being so easily brushed aside.

Kai was an attractive man, and he'd spent a lifetime honing his charm. Romantic rejection wasn't a plight he'd faced often; this ambiguous dismissal was almost worse. Ilsa had already returned to her screens, and the deliberate blankness—a poker face Kai himself had helped her perfect—gave no indication at all of what she might be feeling beneath the surface.

He had no choice but to walk away, leaving his confession to hover between them until the job was done. Awkwardly, and with heavy reluctance, Kai left Ilsa's room. He flinched at the hiss of the door closing behind him.

When Ilsa told him, later the same evening, that she'd broken through to the information she needed, Kai felt a fragment of relief. Though the fact changed nothing, it was reassuring to learn she hadn't been exaggerating when she said she was close. That night Ilsa summoned Kai and Dantes both, excitement and success in the bright tone of her voice.

Her room was lit garishly when Kai arrived to find Ilsa and Dantes sitting on either side of the cluttered desk. Evening sunlight slanted through open windows, leaving the air uncomfortably warm. The room was more spacious than the berths they'd been cramming themselves into one after another over the past few days, and Kai realized there was a third chair by the foot of the bed. He grabbed it and dragged it near the desk, then spun it so he could sit backwards and cross his arms over the back.

"You found her?" Dantes sounded hopeful, but also clearly braced for disappointment.

"No," Ilsa admitted. "But I figured out where all her money went. After passing through dummy accounts and short term investments and backdoors, nearly all the funds ended up in one place. A small company with its base of operations on Praxica VI."

"And the name of this company?" Dantes pressed with an air of impatience.

"The Roy Vis Medica Group," Ilsa answered, and even Kai's eyes went wide at the name.

"That's no small company," Kai protested, his expression mirroring the shock on Dantes's face. "That's one of the largest pharmaceutical conglomerates in the entire quadrant. Even *I've* heard of Roy Vis."

"It's grown a bit since that initial investment," Ilsa conceded, glancing back and forth between the two members of her startled audience. "It was just a tiny research lab during the war. Vis Medica. But the sudden influx of capital allowed them to expand and compete on a wider scale once the war ended."

Kai could well imagine. By the time the Alliance had finally driven off the seemingly endless swathe of invaders, most of the existing corporate superpowers had been taken down a notch. While a well-placed few like Dantes had come out ahead of the game, most suffered drastic losses in their business interests. Attrition, compromised trade routes, communications blackouts, and supply shortages had done immeasurable damage to the galactic economy, even in sectors that managed to avoid outright violence. The changing terrain would have provided perfect opportunity for an emerging player with funds to burn.

Kai turned to Dantes. "Had your company dealt with Vis Medica previously? Maybe there's some preexisting connection."

Dantes shook his head in a firm negative. "I remember them coming almost out of nowhere after the war. I'd never heard of them before they started marketing to multiple sectors. They weren't exactly in my sphere before that. Praxica VI isn't a close neighbor to any of my holdings."

Kai readily accepted this. Praxica VI wasn't a close neighbor to any of the places they'd traveled so far, either. Assuming a direct flight, it would still take them nearly two weeks to make the journey from Lanniah Ceti Three to the Praxica system. That was no hop-skip-jump. That was real distance.

"So we're operating under the assumption that Abigail is involved with this company?" Kai glanced at Ilsa over the tops of her clustered screens.

"Not necessarily." The quick look Ilsa threw at Dantes before dropping her eyes seemed strangely furtive, but her hesitation made sense when she admitted, "At this point in the data stream, I've lost all track of Abigail. Until near the end, I could still see her fingerprints on every transaction, but by the time the money flows into the pharmaceutical company, there's no sign of her."

Dantes's brow knitted and his mouth turned down at one corner. "How is that possible?"

Ilsa tapped a quick sequence into the bottom corner of one screen, then turned it so Kai and Dantes could look. Text only, a screen full to overflowing with what looked like personal information.

"The final investments were made by this woman. Tullia Roy." Ilsa pointed to a section of screen that seemed to provide some kind of corporate timeline, including the change of the pharmaceutical company's name from Vis Medica to the Roy Vis Medica Group. "She may have already been involved in the company in some capacity. Early corporate records are incomplete, so I can't be sure. But the mass investment of new capital was essentially a buyout. Roy took over operations and began making changes almost immediately. She turned the company into one of the most powerful economic engines in the entire sector, and she did it in under two years."

"Impressive as this is," Dantes interrupted, unclenching his jaw to speak, "I'm more interested in finding out how this woman got her hands on my daughter's money."

"That's what worries me," Ilsa admitted. "The money seems to have changed hands abruptly. One second I was following Abigail's trail, the next I was looking at completely different accounts. I did some digging, and this Tullia Roy doesn't exactly cut a reassuring history. What little I could learn about her comes from sources so scattered I can't put together a coherent picture." She pointed to the screen still facing Dantes. "That's as complete a bio as I could construct, and there are dozens of holes in the timeline, not to mention a suspicious lack of photo identification. Whatever she was up to before Roy Vis Medica, I'd bet hard credits it was shady business."

Except shady business was only one possible reason for such a fractured history, and when Kai raised his eyes from the screen, he found Ilsa watching him pointedly. Kai didn't need her wordless admonition to hold his tongue. He kept his thoughts to himself as the screen finished scrolling through information and then stilled.

"And Abigail?" Dantes pressed. "How does this get us any closer to finding my daughter?"

"It doesn't," Kai said, deliberately drawing Dantes's attention. Kai exchanged a quick glance with Ilsa, a split second of perfect understanding, and she nodded at him to continue. Kai forced himself to meet Dantes's glower and explain, "If the digital trail has run cold, there's only one way to find out what happened to Abigail. We need to talk to the only person who might know."

"Tullia Roy." The hard edges of anger didn't soften from Dantes's face, but they shifted inward so that Kai no longer felt trapped at the center of the man's displeasure.

Kai nodded. "She's the one who ended up with Abigail's money. It stands to reason that she and Abigail crossed paths while your daughter was in hiding. Obviously there's no guarantee she'll help us willingly, but if anyone can point us in the right direction, it will be her."

Dantes stood, and there was renewed impatience in the stiff line of his posture. "I'll book passage to the Praxica system immediately." It was a blatant breach of protocol. Their contract stated Kai and Ilsa had final say in all travel arrangements, and Dantes had so far abided those terms without complaint.

Dantes didn't wait to see if Kai and Ilsa agreed with his announcement now, and Kai said nothing to interrupt his sudden retreat. A quick glance confirmed for Kai that Ilsa didn't intend to protest either. Neither spoke as Dantes removed himself from the room with all possible speed, rushing to see the business done.

After Dantes was gone, Kai turned to Ilsa and asked, "What do you really think?"

"I don't know what to think. Nothing's adding up the way it should, and when I try to dig deeper, the data just isn't *there*."

More quietly Kai asked, "Do you think Abigail is still alive?"

"Maybe." Ilsa scowled and began shutting her screens down one by one, methodical ritual in every tap and swipe. "I mean, I goddamn *hope* so. It's possible Abigail met Roy on the run and handed over her resources willingly in exchange for protection or some other consideration."

"Or maybe Abigail *is* Tullia Roy," Kai said. Valiant optimism made him add, "Just because there's been no sign of her doesn't prove something awful happened. Hell, for all we know, she could be avoiding her father."

Ilsa's scowl deepened. "You think I haven't considered the possibility?" She paused as the last screen fell dark, and for just a moment, she closed her eyes, her face smoothing into a calmer expression by force of will. When she opened them again, they were still bright with frustration. "The war's been over for three years. Why should Abigail Dantes still be in hiding?"

Kai peered at Ilsa for a long moment, until understanding hit him. "You have a different theory. But you don't like it."

Ilsa crossed her arms and leaned back in her chair. "Tullia Roy didn't become a player in this drama until well after Helena Kanne disappeared."

Kai blinked in unhappy surprise. "You're saying Helena found Abigail after all."

"I'm saying it's possible." Ilsa breathed a quiet sigh, uncrossing her arms and slouching forward to brace her elbows on the desk. "I've got a bad goddamn feeling about all this. I should be able to find solid information about Tullia Roy. If she's someone trying to protect Abigail Dantes, there should be a connection for me to trace. If she's

Abigail, she's done too good a job covering her tracks. And if she's Helena Kanne, then God only knows what we'll find at the end of this trail. I'm trying not to assume the worst when there are so many possible explanations."

"You don't have to assume the worst to prepare for it."

Ilsa's fierce expression softened, and she shook her head almost sadly. "I know. I just wish this search weren't starting to feel like a murder investigation. I don't want Abigail to be dead. I want to reunite her with her father." She shrugged helplessly. "I may not like Dantes very much, but I don't want to see him bury his only child."

Kai reached forward and covered her hand on the desk, giving it a sympathetic squeeze. The smile he offered felt sad on his face, and he wished he could join her in hanging onto hope by simple force of will.

"We'll find her," he promised. "One way or another, we'll find her." And if Abigail Dantes was dead, then Kai silently vowed they would see justice done.

CHAPTER SIX

The *Keau* was more passenger liner than transport frigate, which should have made a pleasant change of pace. It *was* nice, Ilsa conceded, having the illusion of scenery behind panel screens masquerading as windows. There was nothing convincing about the illusion itself—the images presented were always of planet-side vistas, the better to keep passengers calm and at ease—but she found it pleasant just the same. There were even a handful of small botanical gardens scattered about the ship. Hydroponics mostly, but they offered a generous arrangement of honest greenery and fresh air.

After the first couple days en route, she had to admit there was truly nothing more she could unearth about Tullia Roy. Ilsa spent most of her wakeful hours in a corner of a garden after that. The benches were uncomfortable, meant to offer the appearance of hospitality while actually designed to discourage people from lingering.

But Ilsa had great patience for discomfort, especially when it meant spending the bulk of the journey pretending she wasn't in space at all.

Kai joined her occasionally, or sought her out to beg company in the commissary. He didn't once broach the topic of having kissed her on Depsis, but it was painfully obvious he wanted to return to the topic. Ilsa knew him too well not to notice the edge of impatience barely concealed beneath his easy exterior. Anxiety caught at her insides when she considered the fact that this reprieve was only temporary. The conversation was far from complete, and Ilsa knew she'd left the door wide open for Kai to approach her again once they found Abigail Dantes.

Though she did her best not to remember the wounded surprise on his face, she found it difficult to think of anything else. Little as Ilsa relished the thought of hurting her partner and best friend, she couldn't imagine any other result.

The *Keau* put into port at the largest way station of Praxica's neighboring solar system, where every flight they tried to reserve was already overbooked. Only after an irritable layover and some serious negotiating did Kai manage to convince a cargo transport to carry them the rest of the way.

At least it would be a short trip. Behind the cargo hold there were extra crew seats, with all the necessary harnesses and safety features. The accommodations were tight and claustrophobic, worse by far than anything Ilsa had experienced in recent memory. She spent the journey with her eyes closed, ignoring the occasional bursts of pointless conversation between her two companions, and counting down every moment until arrival.

Praxica VI had thirteen separate spaceports, not counting the two located on its largest moons. Dantes paid the *Keau*'s captain extra to put down at Cita Miri, third largest city on the planet's surface and home to Roy Vis Medica's primary headquarters. Ilsa hadn't been able to pin down an address for the woman herself, so if they were going to find Tullia Roy, then this was where they needed to start.

Once disembarked and settled in fresh rooms, Ilsa used several backdoor traces to access Roy Vis Medica's central terminal. She covered her tracks along the way, wanting to be sure no one could trace her efforts back to a physical location. The hostelry she and Kai had chosen, to Dantes's reluctant agreement, stood near the heart of the city. The location was strategically perfect for digital access, but otherwise it wasn't ideal. She didn't relish the thought of having to book a hasty retreat so far from the nearest port.

At least here, practically on Roy Vis's doorstep, Ilsa could dig deeper. Within twenty minutes, she discovered that Tullia Roy *was* in Cita Miri, scheduled to remain in the city for at least three days. Another ten minutes and Ilsa managed to place a meeting on the corporate calendar for the very next day, under the guise of a sales pitch. False credentials for Ilsa and Kai would keep security at bay, and with any luck, only Tullia Roy would be in attendance at the meeting.

It could still be dangerous. Whether Roy was Helena Kanne or not, if she *had* killed Abigail Dantes, she wasn't likely to confess and turn herself in quietly. Ilsa had her gun, assuming her falsified credentials kept security from searching her too closely. She also had the element of surprise on her side. But there was no surety all these advantages would be enough, and Ilsa remained anxious about the hazardous unknown.

The three met in Kai's room this time, all bracing for the next—perhaps final—step in their search. Ilsa threw Kai a querying look, and Kai met her with an expression both grim and wordless. Confirmation and agreement. With one will between them, they turned and informed Dantes that he would not be accompanying them to the offices of the Roy Vis Medica Group.

"The hell I'm not!" Raw anger raised Dantes's voice almost to a shout. "You work for *me*. I'm not staying behind while you go off and blow the one chance I've got at finding Abigail."

Ilsa rankled at the insult, but beside her, she could tell Kai had taken the words even harder. Already standing, he straightened to his full height and clenched his hands at his sides. There was an unmistakable threat of violence in the tense line of his shoulders. Ilsa was reasonably confident he wouldn't hit a client—even one who had just disparaged their abilities so carelessly—but she reached for him anyway. He steadied beneath the hand she set on his arm, subsiding and letting Ilsa take the lead.

"Mr. Dantes." She spoke evenly despite the anger beneath her own skin. "You hired us to do a job. You signed a contract that says we do the job our way. We've allowed you to join our search, but we won't let you interfere with our methods. This isn't negotiable. You *will* wait here tomorrow while we follow this lead, and we'll report back to you with everything we learn."

For a taut moment, she feared Dantes would argue. There was little they could do if he continued to insist. They had no leverage. They could refuse to perform the contract, but to what purpose? They'd already guided Dantes this far. Refusing to finish the job wouldn't prevent him digging deeper on his own, but it *would* give him grounds for withholding their fee. They could agree to his terms, but Ilsa bristled at the thought. She refused to let her own actions put a client directly in the potential line of fire, even if that client had more than once proven himself a stubborn bully.

Finally Dantes deflated, nodded, and Ilsa breathed easily again.

She spared a glance toward Kai and wished, fleetingly, that she could convince *him* to stay behind too. Images of his blood, the too-deep gash in his injured shoulder, were still fresh in her mind. Her every instinct screamed at her to protect and keep him out of harm's way.

But it wasn't her job to protect Kai. They were partners—they watched each other's backs—and any danger they faced, they faced together, whether Ilsa liked it or not.

*

Kai woke at an unnatural hour the next morning. He'd set no alarm the night before, well aware he wouldn't need it. The excess of nerves and energy beneath his skin roused him early, eager to finally have an outlet. After days of standing uselessly on the sidelines, Kai was anxious to get his hands dirty again. Confronting Tullia Roy was the necessary conclusion to the search that had brought them to Praxica VI. His gut told him they were about to learn what had happened to Abigail Dantes, one way or another.

Kai waited as long as he could bear before barging in on Ilsa, their old patterns restored now that other complications had been put on hold. He found her dressed and ready to go, checking the charge on her gun before slipping the discreet weapon into the side of her boot. She'd dressed in a style that managed to look both practical and professional. Stiff creases pressed into gray pants, and the short sleeves of her blouse wouldn't hamper her movements if things got interesting.

Kai had tried for a similar effect, but with significantly less success. His dark clothes made him look more intimidating than professional, and he had to concede that this time he really did look the part of bodyguard rather than partner.

"Ready?" Ilsa picked up a jacket with longer sleeves, but draped it over one arm instead of putting it on. As a prop it was effective, dark fabric that could be anything. If she actually donned the garment, its simple style would broadcast clearly that she wasn't at all the sales executive her documents claimed.

"Ready," Kai agreed and followed her out the door.

He moved beside her along the hall, into the lift, through the lobby. They squinted in unison at the too-bright sky that stretched cloudless and imposing overhead. Despite the painful glare of the sun, the air was almost uncomfortably cool, and Kai glanced at Ilsa's bare arms with raised eyebrows. She raised a single brow in return and gave a careless shrug. If she was cold, the fact clearly didn't trouble her any more than the bright sun or sporadic wind.

"We should catch a transport," Ilsa murmured, glancing down the street. "The weather can change in a heartbeat here, and if we're caught in the rain we won't look the part well enough to get past security."

Kai glanced down the street. Dusty walkways and skinny buildings climbed to staggering heights, and he had difficulty imagining rain. There was a red sheen to both stone and metal in every direction, and the sharp glint of fewer windows than he might have expected on the towering edifices along the road. He'd studied a map the night before, and he knew exactly where they needed to go, but Roy Vis was at least a dozen blocks away. Even without the improbable threat of rain, they should hire transport to cover the distance.

A rattling hover cab carried them to their destination in a short matter of minutes. The cab parked beside the looming facade of a truly mammoth building. Three sets of double doors faced the street, each at least twenty feet tall. Artful patchworks of colored glass comprised each door, and the panels were set into seams that allowed the doors to slide apart automatically for anyone who approached.

Despite Kai's earlier skepticism, the weather *had* turned nastier in just a few minutes' travel.

The chill breeze had transformed into a strong wind, carrying ominous clouds across the sky and bathing the city in dull grays. The rain began just as Kai finished paying the driver, counting half a dozen credit chips into a furred and padded palm. There was a faint trickle of moisture as he and Ilsa darted from the cab to the narrow overhang fronting the building, and they reached cover just in time.

Then the deluge began. The deafening clatter opened up precisely as Kai and Ilsa slipped through the leftmost set of doors.

"See?" Ilsa murmured smugly. The doors slipped silently shut behind them, leaving only a distorted glimpse of the sudden rainfall outside. Kai snorted. He hadn't spoken his incredulity aloud, but of course Ilsa had read it on his face. He glanced about the lobby instead of acknowledging her triumph.

The building's elegant entry hall was enormous. Vaulted ceilings towered so tall Kai had to crane his neck to see the golden clusters of artificial lights high above. Nearer to ground level there were walls of smooth stone, not marble but something very like it, and a pristine floor to match. Wherever corners jutted inwards there stood massive pillars. The sculpted columns must have cost more money than Kai could fathom, let alone count.

He expected a prominent security checkpoint, but there was only open floor leading to a tall wooden desk that spanned the entire back wall.

Before he could comment on the strangeness, three slickly-dressed security agents approached and cornered them near the doors. All three wore suits in a human style, though not a single one of the three agents fit that description. Two had the same shaggy, clean-furred look of the driver from the hover cab. The third had the eerily smooth, pale and featureless skin of an Aian Vere.

"Is there a problem?" Ilsa pitched her voice with confident authority even as she kept her tone low to avoid drawing extra attention. It was an impressive balance. It was also one in which Kai took especial pride, as he'd spent several months coaching her on it at the beginning of their partnership.

"No problem, sir," the Aian answered in a smooth hiss. "Newcomers must submit to standard security protocols. No inconvenience intended. If you would please follow?"

"Of course." Ilsa threw Kai a glance, and Kai offered an imperceptible nod in turn. There was nothing suspicious about this turn of events. It made a great deal more sense than the apparent lack of security he had first supposed. Kai kept his mouth shut as he followed Ilsa and the three security agents into a small room off the main lobby. Elaborate scanners and sensor equipment lined the far wall, but the trio of agents made no move toward any of the showy apparatus. They seemed content to use more traditional methods.

There was still a chance they would discover Ilsa's weapon, but it was hardly uncommon for businesswomen to travel armed. Kai's main fear of discovery rested on the fact that if security found the weapon, they would confiscate it, leaving Kai and Ilsa to face Tullia Roy at a disadvantage.

But the security agents did only the most cursory check of Ilsa's person, patting down the jacket folded over her arms, making her turn out her pockets. They didn't discover the gun tucked low in Ilsa's boot.

By comparison, they spent what felt like an eternity searching Kai. They patted him down with an admirable thoroughness that would surely have turned up any weapons if he were carrying. As it was, they came away empty-handed, exchanging nods between themselves as though silently congratulating each other for a job skillfully accomplished.

"Well," the Aian said. "Have you an appointment?"

Ilsa pulled a portable data screen from the pocket of her folded jacket and tapped the corner before handing it over for the agents to inspect. Kai assumed it contained both their falsified identification and proof of the meeting Ilsa had scheduled on the Roy Vis Medica system. The agents passed the screen between themselves for a moment, peering closely, before handing it back with identical nods.

"Here you are then, sir." The Aian handed Ilsa two small visitor badges, the kind that looked like inexpensive name plates but would affix to any fabric and most metals once activated. "These will allow you to enter the lifts and access the corporate offices on the upper floors. Please return them when your business is concluded. If you attempt to leave the premises without returning them, you will trigger automatic security measures."

"Understood." Ilsa affixed her own badge before handing the second to Kai. She ignored him as he attached the badge to the front of his dark shirt.

Security directed them to a hall that ran behind the foyer's back wall, where a sequence of lifts waited in a precise row. Kai and Ilsa bypassed the wide desk and rounded the corner into the hall as instructed. They waited amid a milling handful of people, mostly employees who paid them no mind at all. By maneuvering and a hint of luck, Kai and Ilsa managed to secure a lift to themselves, and Kai drew a steadying breath as the opaque doors slid shut.

"Tullia Roy's office is on the seventy-third floor," Ilsa said as she selected their destination. The lift felt like it was hanging completely motionless, but the ping of lights told Kai they were rising quickly through the tall building. Ilsa continued, "If we meet anyone in the hall, let me do the talking. But once we've got Roy cornered, she's all yours."

"This might get ugly," Kai pointed out. The warning was unnecessary, but it felt important to say the words aloud. Grounding. Conspiratorial. Ilsa threw him an exasperated look, but Kai only grinned at her. When the final floor pinged and the door to the lift slid open, Kai waited for Ilsa to exit first, then followed a step behind as befitted a bodyguard or assistant, whichever he was supposed to be.

There were fewer people on this floor. The handful they passed were either hard at work or hurrying along the hall too quickly to bother acknowledging the visitors in their midst. By the time Kai and Ilsa reached the grand suite of offices at the end of the hall—the entrance demarcated by a tall plaque proclaiming Tullia Roy's name in nine different languages—there was no one in sight at all. Kai and Ilsa slipped through the main door without apparent hurry, maintaining their roles for the sake of the security camera Ilsa pointed out with a subtle nod.

The first room was a lobby, sleek and plush and eerily empty. A tidy desk occupied one end of the airy space, standing like an unmanned sentry post beside the hall that led to the business offices themselves. There should have been an admin at that desk, especially at this hour on a standard business day, and Kai slowed his pace as his senses rose to high alert. Beside him, Ilsa tensed, fingers flexing at her sides as though itching for a weapon. She didn't reach for her gun, though, and a moment later she let Kai lead the way around the corner and down the empty hall.

There were no visible security cameras here, but Kai knew better than to assume their absence meant anything. There could be any number of clever hiding places for more discreet monitoring equipment. From the fact that Ilsa kept her weapon out of sight, Kai knew her mind was following the same paths and coming to the exact same conclusions.

Voices reached them as they approached the open door at the end of the hall. The conversation was too quiet to decipher at first. Whoever was in that room was speaking in a deliberate undertone, and Kai couldn't make out any words at all until he took up a position just behind the doorframe.

"You must think you're exceptionally clever." That was Dantes speaking. Kai recognized the familiar sour baritone. "Making me look a complete fool, building an empire out of *my money*. You should have seen this day coming from the first toe you put out of line."

Kai exchanged a glance with Ilsa and found fury on her face to match his own. Slow and cautious, he edged carefully forward to peer around the door frame. Squeezing close beside him, Ilsa did the same, the difference in their heights allowing her to catch a simultaneous glimpse of the scene unfolding in that office.

Rage gripped tight in Kai's chest as his eyes confirmed what his ears were already insisting. There stood Eleazar Dantes, barely ten feet away. Dantes wasn't facing the open door. He wasn't paying the empty hallway any mind at all.

Neither were the two Morann toughs who stood flanking Dantes to left and right, and for a moment, Kai wondered if Dantes had managed to get himself taken hostage. Moranni were fearsome in reputation, a sturdy race known for thick hides and astounding physical strength. They looked more human than most Alliance races, stocky and strong, but with a sickly gray pallor. They also stood a third again as tall as any human. The two standing to either side of Dantes were just shy of having to stoop beneath the office's ceiling. They appeared unarmed, but Kai had no doubt they were both packing a personal arsenal. The matching stiffness of their postures screamed hired muscle so clearly that an observer would have to be asleep to miss the signals.

A second glance quickly dispelled any suspicion that the two Moranni were a threat to Dantes. They weren't even looking at him. They were too busy staring down whomever Dantes was addressing.

Kai realized with a shiver of apprehension that *Dantes* was armed. He held with competent ease the oversized firearm Ilsa had borrowed on Depsis, not aiming directly ahead, but not exactly standing down either. Clearly he had decided to circumvent Kai and Ilsa—to confront Tullia Roy himself—since they'd refused to include him in their plan. Fresh anger surged in Kai's chest, and it was with difficulty that he kept from growling Dantes's name.

Little attention as anyone in the office was paying, Kai chanced leaning farther forward, angling for a look at the rest of the room. The plain office reeked of money, all sleek decor and polished surfaces. Narrow windows were spaced artfully along the two walls Kai could see from his limited vantage point. Minimal furniture filled the room, a couple of perplexing chairs and a slate-colored desk, behind which sat—

Kai blinked and stared. Abigail Dantes sat behind the imposing gray desk. Her hair was darker, her face thinner, but it was unmistakably her. Resigned as he'd been to their worst case scenarios, Kai had difficulty believing the evidence before his own eyes.

The office was empty but for the seated woman and her three uninvited guests.

"Fine." Abigail's voice carried impressive calm. Even from where he stood, Kai could tell she was making a deliberate effort to keep both hands visible. Reacting to her father like a threat. Kai silently conceded there was no other way to read the situation. Abigail sat facing the door, but if she noticed Kai and Ilsa peering past the jamb, she gave no outward sign as she continued, "You've found me. Congratulations. What do you want?"

Kai glanced down and met Ilsa's eyes at an uncomfortably close angle. They exchanged a tightly packed look, and Ilsa nodded. She crouched and drew the gun from her boot, then paused for a fragment of a second.

They needed no signal. The instant Ilsa moved, Kai moved also, two perfectly timed charges into the enormous office. Kai ran the faster, and he didn't slow until he was near enough to twist the weapon from Dantes's grasp.

Then Kai retreated as quickly as he'd closed in, holding the gun like a talisman as the two Morann toughs tensed like coiled springs.

"Don't try it," Ilsa's voice cut grimly through the astounded silence, "or I'll burn a hole through your boss's skull." In his peripheral vision, Kai spotted Ilsa leveling her gun straight at Dantes's head.

The Moranni subsided unhappily, looking to Dantes for instruction.

Distaste shivered beneath Kai's skin as he leveled his stolen gun at the tall mercenary to Dantes's left. Kai had no intention of firing the damn thing, but he wasn't going to forfeit his tactical advantage without attempting to bluff. He held the barrel perfectly steady as he circled away from the threatening trio. His movements made an awkward triangle of opposing forces with himself at the apex, Abigail and Eleazar Dantes at either corner.

Kai stopped only when he reached Ilsa's side. He spoke in a clear, even voice. "If we might politely interrupt. What the *fuck* is going on here?"

Instead of answering, Abigail glared straight at Kai and demanded, "Who the hell are you two? Where is my security detail?"

From his own position, with his wall of hired muscle posturing impatiently to either side, Dantes said, "Your security detail has been... inconvenienced."

Kai threw a startled glance at Ilsa, doing his best to keep his expression blank. Ilsa didn't take her attention off of Dantes or her own carefully aimed weapon, but she didn't have to. From the faint tightening at the corner of her mouth, Kai knew they'd reached identical conclusions: Dantes had at least one other element in the building, completing a sweep even now. The two security agents in the main foyer had unquestionably been Roy Vis Medica employees; impostors would never have allowed Kai and Ilsa into the building in the first place. Dantes must have made his move in the corporate offices first, then sent people to secure the building once he'd attained his objective. It made a certain inevitable sense. Taking on the ground floor security too soon could have tipped his hand and cut off access to the upper levels.

All this Kai deciphered in a fleeting heartbeat. Beside him, Ilsa breathed a barely audible curse.

Dantes's voice turned stony as he tossed a dismissive look toward Kai and Ilsa. "As for these two clowns... they're supposed to be working for me." He looked genuinely offended that they had put themselves in his way, and Kai could almost laugh at the absurdity of the situation. He *would* have laughed if not for the unsettling weight of Dantes's gun in his hands, the gauging stares with which the Moranni regarded him.

Without taking his eyes off the more immediate threat, Kai asked the woman at the desk, "Are you Abigail Dantes?" He already knew the answer; he just needed to hear it aloud.

In his peripheral vision, Kai caught the hard glare she leveled at Eleazar as she answered, "I am."

From Kai's other side, Ilsa announced dryly, "We've been looking for you."

That earned them both a sharp look, surprise and confusion, and a moment later, Abigail rose from her chair. She continued to keep her hands visible—clearly she hadn't decided where Kai and Ilsa's loyalties would ultimately fall and wasn't in the mood to antagonize them—and rounded the desk slowly. She moved to stand at Kai's side opposite Ilsa, though she didn't come too close. Just enough distance remained to prevent Kai reacting defensively to her proximity. Abigail Dantes was clearly a woman who had made it through hairy situations before. Kai hoped that meant she'd keep a level head while they sorted out what to do with this mess.

Abigail wasn't looking at Kai. She was staring directly, furiously, at Dantes. But it was Kai she addressed, her voice cold with rage when she asked, "Is he telling the truth? Do you work for this backstabbing piece of shit?"

"That's no way to speak of your own father." Dantes's retort simmered with malicious amusement, and the tone sent an alarmed twitch along Kai's spine.

Fucking hell. Kai had harbored a slippery feeling about Dantes from the start, but he'd seen no inkling of *this*. He and Ilsa would never have taken the case if Kai had seen such potential in Dantes's character. Now, too late, Kai wondered how he could have misgauged the man so severely. His instincts had never let him down this spectacularly before.

"Shut your *fucking* mouth," Abigail snarled at her father. She didn't sound cool now. She sounded vicious and riled. But she wasn't armed. Only Kai and Ilsa held ready weapons. There had to be a way to pull this situation back from wherever it was careening.

Dantes collected himself. His posture eased, and he crossed his arms imperiously. His gaze darted from Abigail, to Kai, to Ilsa, and back again.

It was on Kai his attention finally settled, and Dantes offered a careless shrug of one shoulder. "I'll admit, I haven't been entirely truthful with you. When Abigail ran away, she absconded with an alarming amount of capital from my private accounts. All I want is what's rightfully mine."

"You murdered my mother for her *money*, you sick bastard. Did you honestly think I'd sit by and let you profit from what you'd done?"

Abigail's words rang through the office like a gunshot, leaving ragged silence in their wake. The accusation hung there, awful and ugly, and again, Kai found himself wondering how he could have looked Dantes in the eye and seen anything good. Selfish malice twisted the man's face now, turning his aspect ugly and grim.

Silence clung through several taut seconds. The weight of Abigail's accusation hung heavy in the air.

Dantes uncrossed his arms and let them fall to his sides. "The High Court dismissed those charges."

There was an unmistakable sneer in Abigail's voice when she retorted, "That doesn't make you any less guilty."

The conviction in Abigail's voice might have been enough to convince Kai on its own, but it was the answering smugness on Dantes's face that proved incontrovertible. Kai's gut twisted with a surge of nausea at the thought of a man murdering his own wife in cold blood, and for what? An inheritance? The fact that Dantes had not only done it, but had gotten away with it, made Kai physically nauseous.

Ilsa muttered a fresh curse, perfect counterpoint to the incredulous anger slinking beneath Kai's skin. Kai drew a breath and tried to steady himself. They needed to call the authorities. They needed to find a way out of here with their skulls intact, but also without letting Eleazar Dantes escape, or worse, succeed at what he'd come for. They had brought him here; it was on their heads if he harmed Abigail now.

Heavy footfalls from the hall jarred Kai from his indecision, and he and Ilsa both turned toward the sound.

They turned too late. Three Moranni stormed through the door with guns drawn, bringing the total count of Dantes's hired muscle to five. Their arrival gave the two hulks flanking Eleazar the chance they needed to draw weapons. A flash of metal and practiced movement, and abruptly all five were sporting oversized charge rifles. The rifles looked more like electrical canons than handguns, and Kai couldn't fathom how the mercenaries had hidden those weapons beneath the drab lines of their jackets.

Two of the muzzles were aimed eloquently at Kai. The other three at Ilsa. There was no room at all to maneuver. Dantes strode forward, all casual bravado, and Kai reluctantly relinquished the gun. Beside him, Ilsa surrendered her weapon to Dantes as well. She wore a sullen look, her dark eyes burning with wrath.

"Thank you," Dantes breezed, satisfaction in every step as he took up his position between the first two Moranni. "Now. Down to business, I think?" He turned on his daughter, and though he didn't raise either of the weapons to aim, there was no subtlety at all in the way he held both his own gun and Ilsa's confiscated weapon. Casually, one in each hand. An obvious threat. "Abigail. I don't think I need to explain how disappointed I am in you. I've expended a great deal of time and money tracking you down, never mind the funds you stole."

Abigail kept silent, and Kai couldn't guess what expression she wore. He didn't dare try to find out. He was too concerned about the live weapons pointed directly at his head.

"Given that every penny you invested in this company belongs to me," Dantes continued, letting his gaze take in the office with the assessing air of ownership, "it's clear that Roy Vis Medica *also* belongs to me. No court or arbiter could find otherwise. Therefore, I will be taking *immediate* control of my new holdings. And *you* will return home with me, under solitary guard." His eyes narrowed and his mouth thinned to a flat line. "If you are very, *very* lucky, you might see daylight again this century. If you continue to defy me, you'll learn first hand what became of your meddlesome aunt."

Despite his wiser instincts, Kai turned to catch sight of Abigail's stricken face in the wake of these words. Wounded rage and a first hint of fear warred across her expression before settling into a seething mask.

Kai's fists clenched uselessly at his sides, and even if he'd wanted to speak, he couldn't have summoned the means. His throat was too tight, his jaw firmly clenched. When he faced forward once more, he ached with how desperately he wanted to punch the smug sneer off Eleazar Dantes's face.

He had never hated anyone before. It was a slick, oily feeling, and he didn't like it one bit.

Dantes's focus shifted away from Abigail at last, sliding past Kai to land on Ilsa. "As for you two." Dantes's voice softened unkindly. "I *had* intended to pay you for your services and let you walk away. But I'm afraid you've rendered yourselves expendable."

Protest clenched in Kai's chest, and he struggled to swallow past the disbelieving outrage trying to climb up his throat. That trembling sensation of hatred intensified to a keen, vibrant edge. It felt all the worse for the weight of futility; there was nothing he could do as he and Ilsa were forced to their knees by hired thugs. A surge of denial rose and left the bitter taste of bile at the back of Kai's throat. His hands were bound behind him, and he knew the same was being done to Ilsa close by. They were still facing down five guns between them.

Dantes had made no move to take aim himself, but he damn well didn't need to. This was no intimidation ploy.

This was an execution.

Kai twisted his gaze away from the black-barreled muzzles. If he was about to die, he wouldn't let Eleazar Dantes be the last thing he saw. It was a relief to find Ilsa meeting his eyes with a steady strength Kai wished he could share.

"Last words?" Dantes taunted. When neither Kai nor Ilsa gave even a flinch of acknowledgment, he tutted, "All right then. Boys?"

The five rifles hummed, charges cycling as power built in their chambers. Kai's skin tingled. Ilsa looked collected and calm, as quietly furious as Kai had ever seen her.

Then all five guns clicked as triggers were pulled, and Kai's entire body clenched.

The explosive discharge didn't come. No rush of heat, no burst of pain and power and agony. Kai still knelt upright. Ilsa was still wide-eyed and whole beside him. They hadn't disintegrated in the simultaneous blast of five high-powered charge rifles.

"What the fuck are you doing?" Dantes demanded of his thugs. "*Fire*."

"We did, sir," one of them protested, small mouth forming the Terran-standard syllables awkwardly.

Dantes muttered beneath his breath and tucked Ilsa's weapon in a pocket in order to take aim with his own gun.

He concentrated on Kai first, leveled his shot, then exhaled and fired. Kai flinched—he couldn't help it—but again there came only the muted click of a trigger followed by dull silence.

"*No*," Dantes snarled, throwing his gun to the floor and drawing Ilsa's. The small weapon looked miniature in his large hand. It too failed to discharge.

Dantes's face had gone violently scarlet in a few short seconds, and he looked to be choking on the force of his anger. He opened his mouth. To curse, to demand an explanation, to order his goons to finish them off the hard way. Kai honestly couldn't tell which was more likely, and no sound came out as Dantes's jaw worked.

"Who's the fool now, *Father*?"

Dantes whirled, glaring so fiercely Kai was surprised the austere office walls didn't ignite under the assault. Kai risked a turn of his head, but Abigail no longer stood anywhere near him. She must have moved during the botched murder attempt. She'd reclaimed her position behind the desk, an implacable expression on her narrow face.

Held straight out before her, steadied in both hands, was a weapon Kai recognized as a slug-loaded manual action firearm. Not an antique, but certainly outdated. Kai couldn't remember the last time he'd seen one.

Abigail's smile was so grim Kai honestly couldn't decide whether to be heartened or terrified.

In a placid voice she explained, "Energy-based weapons won't work in this office. Or anywhere else on this floor. There's a singh-stratum damping field preventing your guns from discharging." She aimed the compact piece in her own hand directly at Dantes, and her macabre smile slipped away to cold rage. "The field isn't a physical barrier. It won't stop a bullet. And you're a goddamn fool if you think disabling my internal security squad leaves me helpless."

With a shudder and screech, the narrow windows along the wall behind the desk shattered inward. The abrupt change of air pressure echoed painful in Kai's ears, and he clenched his eyes shut against the dusty glitter of vaporized material raining down. He opened them again to disorientation. Behind him, his wrists twisted futilely in their bindings.

The empty window frames were barely wide enough for a grown man to pass through, but an entire team was slipping through them just the same. One by one, a dozen armed figures in protective gear appeared as if by magic. They slithered into the office, dropping from heavy cables and quickly surrounding the intruders. They moved with practiced efficiency, disarming and restraining the Morann thugs without delay.

At first, Kai couldn't place the howl of rage he heard cutting through the chaos. There was too much noise, too much movement crammed into too small a space. The large office seemed tiny now, full to bursting with the rescue forces Abigail had somehow summoned.

By the time Kai identified the source of the sound, Dantes was already in motion. He was lunging toward the desk—toward his daughter—and the glint of a blade flashed in his grip.

Abigail's weapon was still in her hand, but she made no move to fire, even as her eyes widened and she tried to retreat out of range. The wall at her back left nowhere to go.

A gunshot rang in Kai's ears and he saw Dantes fall.

Dantes landed hard just short of the desk, a spray of blood glazing the floor in patterned red. He was dead by the time he hit the ground. Abigail's eyes flew to the security agent who had fired the shot, and the office fell instantly silent. Scuffling ceased, voices quieted, action halted in the wake of that single bullet.

"Get out," Abigail whispered over the sudden stillness. "Everyone. Out. *Now.*"

The security detail began to disperse, taking the Morann toughs with them. Two guards remained, Gaiminn women with clear eyes and uncertain expressions on their faces. They looked to Abigail with obvious deference.

"What about those two?" one of them asked.

Abigail glanced down at Kai and Ilsa with the obvious surprise of someone who'd forgotten there were still loose ends to deal with. Kai prayed her idea of tying up loose ends differed from her father's.

"Cut them loose," Abigail answered at last. "And leave them here. This is a private conversation."

There was a brief commotion as the two security agents obeyed her commands. Kai flexed his hands when they were free, willing his circulation to dispel the painful pins and needles of returning sensation. When Ilsa was also free, Kai caught her in a crushing hug, drawing his first real breath since Dantes had ordered them shot. After an unsteady moment, Ilsa's arms wrapped around his waist, clutching him back in turn. She was shaking almost as hard as he was.

The quiet click of the door reminded Kai they still had uncomfortable business before them, and he unwrapped himself from Ilsa with reluctance. The office was a disaster, but it had emptied of armed personnel. Dantes's body was gone, too. Only the darkening splatter of blood on the floor gave any indication of where he'd fallen.

Abigail Dantes had emerged from behind her desk to stare at that bloody spot. She looked entirely composed but for the silent tears streaking her perfectly blank face. After a moment, she wiped her eyes with one sleeve. She turned to offer a hand up first to Ilsa, then Kai.

She regarded them in pained silence for so long Kai started wondering if she was waiting for them to make the first move.

Finally, Abigail spoke, the measured pragmatism in her words belied by the sheen of tears still gathered in her eyes. "You'll do me a lot of damage if you share this story publicly."

"It's not our story to share," Ilsa answered for both herself and Kai. She spoke the words with an honest intensity that Abigail Dantes surely must have heard and believed.

Just in case the simple assertion wasn't enough, Kai added, more quietly and with enormous care, "Miss Roy, all our cases are confidential. No matter the outcome." The use of her adopted name was a calculated concession, a promise of complete discretion. From the softening of Abigail's stern face, she took his meaning.

"Thank you," she said. "But you might as well call me Miss Dantes. I've got no reason to hide now, and *every* reason to wish myself recognized as my father's heir."

"I'm sorry," Kai murmured. He meant it sincerely. His own anger at Dantes's betrayal—his own moment of genuine hate—didn't diminish his sympathy for a woman who had just lost her father, monstrous as the man might have been.

Abigail regarded Kai without speaking for several seconds before drawing a deep breath and declaring, "You can both go. I won't keep you any longer. I'll signal security to let you leave."

When Abigail turned her back on them in dismissal, Kai followed Ilsa. The floor crunched strangely beneath every step, granulated matter caught in the thin carpet. They reached the door, and Kai's legs went shaky with relief at the revelation that they were going to make it out of this building whole and unhurt.

Abigail's voice stopped them at the threshold. "Send me an invoice for your services. I'll see my father's debts settled."

Kai turned. He didn't bother to keep the surprise from his face. "You intend to pay us? After all this?"

From her desk, seated once more in the stiff-looking chair with its tall back and newly tarnished upholstery, Abigail answered levelly, "Yes. I do."

CHAPTER SEVEN

Ilsa reclaimed her gun from Abigail's security detachment, then handed over her visitor's badge. She assumed Kai would do the same but didn't wait to find out, hurrying for the lifts as quickly as she could without looking like she was running from a crime scene. She knew Kai was keeping pace despite the silence permeating the hall. She trusted that he would be at most a step behind her. The scant few employees they'd passed on their way in were long gone, hopefully warned off or scared away by the ruckus.

She stubbornly didn't speak as she and Kai navigated the building. Behind her, Kai kept equally quiet.

On the ground floor, at the front doors with their panes of colored glass, Ilsa paused and gave Kai a wordless once-over. Her eyes ran him up and down, checking for blood or any other evidence of the ordeal they'd just walked away from. The thorough sweep of his eyes told her Kai was returning the favor, and a moment later, the tiny shake of his head confirmed that she was clear. Ilsa tucked her gun out of sight and stepped away, triggering the door, then strode stiffly across the threshold.

It wasn't raining anymore.

They walked three blocks before waving down a cab, then asked the driver to take a circuitous path back to their hostel. Seated and finally still, Ilsa could feel excess adrenaline turning sour beneath her skin. Her limbs, already shaky, trembled in the cool cab.

Kai was restless in the seat beside her. She could sense a familiar protectiveness in his posture, and in the furtive glances he kept throwing her way. At the slightest invitation, he would slip an arm about her shoulders and tuck her against his side. He'd done it a hundred times before, in situations far less overwhelming than this.

Normally Ilsa would welcome the reassurance of contact. This time she kept her expression stiff, her shoulders tight, broadcasting without words that she didn't want to be touched. Kai eventually subsided, slouching into his seat with a look of defeat.

Unexpected anger brushed behind Ilsa's ribs as she observed Kai in her peripheral vision. This wasn't anger at Dantes or at the betrayal that had almost gotten them killed, overwhelming as those feelings were. This was a subtler upset that nagged at her, and it took several blocks to decipher where the sensation was coming from.

She was angry at *Kai.* For kissing her. For putting the offer of something more complicated than friendship between them and making Ilsa doubt a closeness she had never wanted to question.

Ilsa *wanted* Kai's arm around her shoulder, damn it. She wanted the tangible assurance that he was whole and unhurt. She wanted to accept comfort in the wake of the ugliness behind them. And she was angry at Kai for making her question what should have been the simplest and most natural gesture.

By the time they reached the building they had checked into with Dantes, Ilsa felt ready to crawl out of her own skin. She settled for disembarking the cab and leaving Kai to pay the fare, making her way into the building before he finished. She gathered her things quickly. They wouldn't be staying here a second longer than necessary, and Ilsa collected her data screens and what few sundries she'd unpacked, tucking them all securely in her rucksack. Her gun she kept at the ready. She slipped it into the left pocket of her long coat, though she prayed she wouldn't need to use it.

She found Kai waiting patiently in the hall. He had donned his well-worn jacket, and his own bag sat propped against one leg.

"I already checked us both out of our rooms," he said. He sounded less certain when he added, "I told them to contact Roy Vis Medica about Dantes's suite. It didn't seem right to evict a dead man, and I thought Abigail might want his things." Unlikely as the possibility sounded, Ilsa knew Kai had made the right choice. Eleazar Dantes had never been their responsibility. It wasn't their job to see to his belongings now that he was gone.

They found a new place to stay, and Ilsa prayed it would only be for one night. This hostel was cheaper, smaller, and practically on top of the main port terminal at the edge of Cita Miri. Ilsa wanted to put Praxica VI and this city behind her as quickly as possible.

She barely paused to toss her bag into her new room before turning right back around and heading for the stairs. Kai hesitated beside his own door and gawped at her with obvious alarm.

"You can't go back out there *now.*" He took a step as though to follow, but fell still instead. "We don't know if Dantes has other allies in the city. We could have been followed."

"I don't care." Ilsa stopped only with reluctance. She was jittery, and the thought of entombing herself in some tiny rented room made her hands fist so tightly her nails dug into her palms. "I'm going to go book us the first available passenger transport out of this system." She wouldn't be particular about the destination, either.

"You can do that from right here," Kai pointed out, and he sounded entirely reasonable. Only the faint crease between his brows gave any hint of the concern Ilsa could read below his calm surface.

"I'd rather do it in person. Cash is more difficult to trace."

"Then I'll come with you." Again Kai moved as if to follow, but this time it was Ilsa's curt reply that stopped him short.

"*No.*"

Kai froze in genuine surprise. "No?"

"No," Ilsa repeated. The narrow hall seemed to be closing in around her, stifling and hot. All she wanted was open air and a few minutes truly alone. Ironic that to achieve what she needed she intended to bury herself in the noisy crowds of the planet's largest port. She leveled a stubborn look at Kai, and her words were too hard to be mistaken for a suggestion when she said, "You can stay here and file our invoice with Roy Vis Medica. I'll be back before you can blink."

The furrow at the center of Kai's brow deepened. "It's not safe to travel alone right now. What if—"

"*I don't care*," Ilsa snapped, louder this time. She closed her eyes for a brief moment, drew a deliberate breath through her nose. Her temper had begun to fray around the edges, and the last thing she wanted was to let careless words damage the already uncertain balance between herself and Kai. When she finally spoke again, she sounded calmer, if barely. "I need to take a walk. Alone. I'm armed, remember? And anyone who might be looking will expect us to lay low. There's no way they'll anticipate an in-person appearance at the main terminal."

Kai didn't look entirely convinced, but he subsided at last. When Ilsa turned once more to retreat, he let her go without protest.

The sky was clear when Ilsa stepped out of the hostel. There were only a handful of people on the narrow street that cut between buildings toward the main thoroughfare. Clusters of storm clouds lingered at the very edge of the horizon, but directly above she saw only vibrant blue and squinting sunlight. The calm arch of unblemished sky.

Normally such a view would have settled Ilsa in her own skin.

Then again, normally she wouldn't be taking in the sight with one hand inside her pocket, the cool of gunmetal brushing her fingers. The rough pavement ground had been patched up one too many times and was in desperate need of a do-over. A mess of puddles scattered along her path, and Ilsa took her time navigating around and between. Her meandering strategy kept her boots mostly dry, even as she maintained a wary eye on her surroundings. The street widened as she walked, the buildings growing shorter as she neared the port terminal with its expansive airfields. There was noise and life, but none of the crowds were heavy enough to make Ilsa anxious. Sporadic as they were, it would be difficult for someone to sneak up on her unnoticed.

Foot traffic grew denser as the spaces between buildings widened, and eventually the expanding road emptied onto a massive street that led directly to the terminal. There were shuttle pods and hovering cabs and a dozen other transports for hire, all of them eager to help shorten the distance. Ilsa bypassed them all and walked the entire route.

She returned the same way once her business was complete, barely noticing the quiet ache in her feet as the road gradually narrowed. By the time she caught sight of the hostel's drab facade, the sun was setting fiercely behind it. Clear sky burned itself into violent pinks and oranges along the horizon, darkening to wild bruises higher above. The building before her didn't look quite so ugly in silhouette as it had only a couple of hours before.

Ilsa took the lift to her floor and stepped into the hall on tired legs.

She froze at the sight of Kai sitting outside her door. His posture was loose. He sat with his knees tucked to his chest and his arms crossed on top of them. He looked like he'd been slouched there the entire time Ilsa had been gone. Waiting for her to return.

Ilsa stared, rigid with surprise. The cautious expression on Kai's face when he turned his head did nothing to dull the wariness creeping through her.

"What are you doing out here?" She took a step forward, then another, one foot in front of the other until she was standing immediately in front of him. Close enough to trip if he stretched his legs across the cramped corridor. She couldn't fathom what he was doing in the hall. Privacy was a concept they hadn't held to for years. It wasn't *them*.

Except maybe it was now. Maybe it needed to be. With an awkward jolt, Ilsa realized there was only one topic that would make Kai behave like this, and she wished she could take her question back. Too late, though. Kai was already answering.

"I wanted to finish that conversation we've been putting off." There was no mistaking what conversation he meant. His gaze held her frozen as he regarded her from the ground, his eyes flashing with tenuous hope and far too much intensity. Ilsa swallowed, her throat gone suddenly dry.

It was shitty timing, but she could hardly fault him for it. They'd both almost died today.

"Come inside." She stepped past him to manually key her access code into the panel beside the door. A rustle of fabric signaled Kai rising to his feet behind her. She stepped inside, Kai at her heels. The room was dark, but it brightened automatically, casting a sedate glow across the confined space. There were no windows to showcase the impressive sunset. Ilsa would have preferred windows. Open sky.

She would make do without them for one night.

There was only one chair in the room, and Ilsa made no move to sit in it. She crossed to the far wall instead, where a squat little bureau sat wedged between the bed and the bathroom door. When she turned around to face Kai, she found him standing uncertainly in the middle of the room.

Ilsa crossed her arms and quirked an expectant eyebrow. She was genuinely surprised he didn't speak first. "What do you want, Kai?" she asked before the silence grew too heavy to break.

He gave a foundering shrug. "I get that you're not thrilled with me, and I'm sorry I made things weird. I just want to know what's going on inside your head right now."

"Inside *my* head?" Ilsa stared, painfully aware of an uninvited tightness gripping her chest. Disbelief caught and held her. If *anyone's* behavior had taken a confusing turn, it was Kai's. Something told her she wouldn't get far trying to convince him of such an obvious truth, though, and she heard herself ask, "Why did you kiss me?"

Kai's face scrunched into a perplexed expression that might have been endearing in a hundred other circumstances. "You know why I kissed you."

"I really don't."

The icy feeling in her chest worsened when Kai's pause stretched into an unsteady quiet. The quiet was both painful and awkward, and Kai seemed a little bit lost when he admitted, "I'm in love with you."

The words landed between them like boulders. That was how they felt to Ilsa, at least: heavy and unwelcome and crushing. The confession blew a mile past her suspicions, and it was with a winded feeling that she retreated a step on shaky legs. When her knees buckled a moment later, she landed hard on the low bureau and had to grasp at the edge for balance. She stared at Kai, wide open and stunned.

She saw his moment of hesitation. A slight shift in balance was all that conveyed his urge to rush to her side. The force of her shock must have stayed him because instead of hurrying forward, he stuffed both hands in his front pockets. He stood there in the center of the room, watching her with hazel eyes gone painfully bright. He still looked lost as he waited for an answer to his confession.

Ilsa summoned her voice with difficulty. "I just assumed you wanted to sleep with me."

"Well... yeah, I mean. I definitely want that, too."

"Kai, I'm not... I don't... You understand that's never going to happen, right?"

"Never?" Kai echoed, doubt on the cusp of heartbreak.

"Never," Ilsa repeated firmly. The crushed agony on his face—there and then hidden in the span of a heartbeat—made her wish there were some other answer she could give him. Guilt twisted behind her ribs, followed by an equal measure of anger, and the two feelings twined into an unhappy knot. It hurt to see the studied blank of Kai's face. The expression cut her almost as deeply as his fleeting wounded look a moment before.

It hurt even more to think that after all these years they could still misunderstand each other so terribly.

Exasperation tinged Ilsa's voice and made her sound defensive when she said, "For God's sake, you're my partner. You're my *best friend.* How was I supposed to know you were looking for more?"

"I wasn't *looking*," Kai protested. The veneer of calm cracked enough to let a corner of hurt show through. "I didn't mean to fall in love with you. It just... happened."

"Kai..." Her eyes cut to the floor with its faded carpet as she tried to sort her thoughts into something coherent enough to explain. From this angle, she could only see Kai from the knees down, his dark trousers and heavy boots, but even that limited snapshot told her he was holding himself completely motionless. Awaiting an unwanted verdict. She forced herself to raise her head, to meet him straight on and speak with warm certainty. "You're the most important person in my life. I care for you. But not like this."

"Then how?" Kai pressed, and the quiet of his voice clawed straight through her defenses.

"Like family," she said. "Like a partner. Like the closest friend I've ever had. Why do we have to sleep together for that to count?" Her voice had risen gradually, from quiet fervor to almost a shout, and she had to bite at her lips to stop from continuing past a point already made.

Kai remained silent for a long time. Seconds stretched into minutes at most, but they felt like a fraught eternity. Ilsa entertained her first inkling of hope when the worst of the thunder passed from Kai's face.

"You have feelings for someone else," he said, and the sliver of hope squeezed away to nothing.

"No." She'd had this conversation before. Dozens of times, each worse than the last. She'd never expected to have it with Kai.

"You're not attracted to men, then?" There was no guile in Kai's expression, and even the sting of rejection seemed to have faded beneath a quizzical need to decipher the situation. That he might be entirely missing the point didn't seem to have occurred to him.

Ilsa unclenched her jaw to answer, "I'm not attracted to anyone."

Kai's brow knitted in renewed confusion. "I don't understand."

Frustration spiked high and hard, and it was with gravel in her voice that Ilsa snapped, "Sex. Romance. I don't need them, and I don't *want* them. Not from you or anyone else. I'm not interested." She couldn't put it more plainly, and she willed him to accept the uncomplicated truth.

Instead he shook his head and asked, "But *why*?"

"Damn it, Kai, there doesn't have to be a reason. This is just me." Her patience was unraveling, her voice rising, and she didn't care. She knew all the arguments, all the answers, all the skewed logic and standard protests. More than anything, she wanted Kai to be smart enough not to follow in those same worn tracks.

Because Kai *was* smart. And he was kind. He had never let her down before. It killed her somewhere deep and secret that he was letting her down now, but she still wasn't entirely surprised when he tripped headlong into the first familiar trap.

"Did something happen?" Kai allowed himself a single forward step as worry became the dominant emotion on his face. "Did someone hurt you?"

"*No,*" Ilsa snarled. Familiarity did nothing to lessen the ache of listening to this script play out, and her hands clenched tighter around the edges of the bureau. Her knuckles paled as her grip squeezed the blood from her fingers.

"Are you sure?" Kai pressed, undeterred. "It's possible you wouldn't remember. Sometimes—"

"Fuck you." Ilsa cut him short with the low chill of her voice. "I'm going to do us both a favor and pretend you didn't just say that to me." The last of her patience snapped so sharply her entire spine straightened, and she glared at Kai with jarring anger.

"But," Kai began, and Ilsa steamrolled straight over him. She couldn't bear to let this disaster play out along the same old pattern.

"No. Just goddamn *stop.* Are you listening to the words coming out of your mouth right now?" There was no more measuring her tone, no more considering her words. There was only wrath and ice—and somewhere quieter, a low sting of betrayal. "Even if someone did hurt me, the fact that *you* want me wouldn't make it your business." She paused to inhale painfully. "And *fuck you* for assuming the only conceivable reason I might not want to sleep with you is *trauma*."

Kai flinched beneath the force of her speech. To his credit, he looked genuinely chastened. For once, Ilsa didn't feel the irrational twinge of guilt. She was far too angry for remorse.

When Kai finally spoke, his tone was conciliatory and too gentle. "I'm just worried about you."

Ilsa snorted and let go of the bureau to cross her arms tightly over her chest. The fire of her temper was stoked too high to let Kai off the hook so easily. "You're not worried about me. You're not even hearing me through your hurt goddamn pride. You think I'm *wrong* somehow just because I'm not giddy at being invited into your bed."

"I didn't say that!" Kai took a single involuntary step toward her before wisely subsiding. "This isn't just about sex."

Ilsa quieted her voice with straining willpower. "I know it's not just sex. But you still aren't hearing me. I've never wanted to be *anyone's* one-and-only." She paused and forced herself to draw a slow breath before finishing, "Not even yours."

"I just want to understand." Kai's voice was impossibly soft, and suddenly hurting in ways that had nothing to do with pride. Ilsa's heart gave an aching pulse, but she kept her expression stern.

"Get out of my room. I'm not going to explain myself again just because you didn't listen the first time."

"Ilsa—"

"I said *get out.*" She rose to her feet in a rush. "And don't come back." Bravado alone kept her steady now. There was a cold lump in her chest that she recognized as her own breaking point, a chill spreading along her sternum and stinging her eyes with the threat of tears. She refused to cry with Kai watching her, but she wouldn't be able to hold herself back much longer.

For an ugly instant, she feared Kai would stand his ground. It was a physical relief when he finally left, disappearing through the door without another word.

Alone, Ilsa sank to the edge of her bed and let herself shake to pieces.

*

Kai wasn't surprised he couldn't find sleep that night.

His restlessness had little to do with fear of delayed retribution from Eleazar Dantes. It wasn't only the deep bite of Ilsa's rejection, either; having his romantic interest shot down hurt far less than the guilt of causing his partner pain.

He'd seen Ilsa angry plenty of times in their seven-year partnership. But he'd never seen a wounded rage like this, and he'd certainly never been right at the epicenter of the event. The strength of her reaction staggered him, and he couldn't keep to his bed through the uncomfortable midnight emptiness. He stayed upright instead. Pacing, thinking, reliving every moment of their exchange. Some of those moments were agony; they were even worse once he cooled down enough to really hear *Ilsa* through his own bruised feelings.

She was right, and his heart gave an unsteady lurch at the revelation. He'd been too busy listening to his own ego to recognize that what she'd said had nothing to do with him. Kai replayed the words that had come out of his own mouth, the questions gone off course, and his chest burned with confusion and regret.

Few things ached like self-awareness come too late.

By the time the chronometer by the door announced dawn's arrival, Kai's head was throbbing with a sullen ache. Three hours later he found it nearly impossible to obey Ilsa's admonition to stay away, when all he wanted was to pound on her door and apologize. At noon he started to wonder if he ought to call the port terminal. Ilsa hadn't told him when their transport would depart, or even where they would be going. Maybe he could learn if there were pending departures booked under any of their half-dozen traveling aliases.

He didn't try to eat. The roil of remorse in his gut made the prospect too unappealing.

Kai was ready to crawl out of his skin by fourteen-hundred when the chime on his door cut through the stifling silence of his rented room.

Ilsa wore a stiff expression when Kai gestured her inside. She shook her head at his offer of the room's sole chair. She opted instead to stand near the door. Her posture was stern, her arms crossed in a defensive stance. She'd bound her hair into a thick braid, and though she wasn't wearing her long coat, she looked dressed to travel. The heavy shadows beneath her eyes suggested she'd spent the night every bit as sleepless as Kai, and the tense line of her shoulders was enough to prevent him from approaching.

"I'm sorry," he said, desperate and sincere and willing Ilsa to look him at him.

When she finally did, he had to fight to stand his ground. There was familiar intensity in her eyes, but the emotion behind them reflected blunted hurt. Kai shivered. He could explain until the galaxy dissolved that he'd been wrong last night, that he hadn't meant to hurt her. But there was too much power in words already spoken, and Kai couldn't undo a harm he still didn't entirely understand.

Ilsa's voice was steady and strong, measured, with the unmistakable air of a well-rehearsed delivery. "I've never been interested in sex, or any of the baggage that comes with it. That doesn't make me wrong inside. It's just how I am."

"I'm sorry." Kai clenched his hands at his sides to keep himself still. "I fucked up."

Ilsa nodded. The worst of the tension eased, but her face still wore a guarded stiffness. She didn't uncross her arms. "You're not my lover, Kai.

You're my best friend. How was I supposed to know you wanted something else?"

"Ilsa, please." Kai's whole body jerked forward a step before he could stop himself. When he fell motionless once more, Ilsa was eyeing him warily. The expression cut straight through him, and his jaw clenched with self-reproach.

She continued to watch him closely, and he knew before she spoke that he wasn't going to like her next words.

"If that's what you need from me, maybe we shouldn't work together."

Denial froze through Kai's blood, sharpened in his veins, narrowed his field of vision until he could see nothing but the set of Ilsa's jaw, the ache in her dark eyes. His skin felt suddenly hot, while cold panic twisted low in his gut.

"I don't," he swore. "I don't need any such thing. I just need you to be my partner." He tried to picture what his life would be without Ilsa, and the only images he could summon were bleak and empty.

There was tightness now around Ilsa's eyes, and her voice sounded strained. "What if I'm not sure I want a partner anymore?"

Kai's knuckles went white as his hands clenched harder. He couldn't find his voice to answer.

Ilsa looked away, toward the door that had brought her. "I thought I knew you so well," she confessed, the words escaping in a rush of feeling. "I thought you were the one person who would never put me in this position. The things you said last night... goddamn it, Kai, I thought I could trust you."

"You *can* trust me," he rasped, staring at her profile. His whole body thrummed with the panic beneath his skin.

"Can I?" Her throat worked in a sharp swallow. "Because I'm not sure anymore. And if I can't trust you, then why am I still here?"

"Because we're a team. Because we need each other."

Ilsa shook her head, and there was resignation in her beautiful face. "I can't do this. I can't just stand beside you and pretend everything's normal."

Kai felt a hot sting behind his eyes, the first prickling threat of tears as he realized, "You came to say goodbye."

Still staring at the door, Ilsa said, "I knew you'd worry if I just disappeared, and... I figure after everything we've been through together, I owe you better than that. I needed to tell you in person."

"Please don't go." Kai did step forward now, deliberately, right to the edge of Ilsa's personal space. He didn't try to touch her, but he let desperation twist his voice into something frantic when he repeated, "Please. We need each other."

Finally, Ilsa looked at him, but there was no hint of reassurance in her exhausted face. "I canceled our joint travel arrangements. You can go wherever you want as long as you don't follow me. I'll be off-planet within the hour."

She stepped away from him, toward the door, and Kai blurted, "Where will you go?"

Ilsa hesitated, hand hovering over the panel that would slide the door open. "I haven't decided yet." Then she pressed the panel and threw him a last look over her shoulder. "So long, Kai. Be safe."

It seemed an eternity before the door slid shut, soundless and unforgiving. With Ilsa gone, Kai slipped to the floor and silently begged the room to stop spinning.

CHAPTER EIGHT

Ilsa boarded the first reputable passenger liner flying out from Praxica VI. She had no particular destination in mind other than *elsewhere*, nor did she care how long it took to get there. Once she'd achieved some distance, she could put out feelers, see about finding a job somewhere planet-bound until she decided what to do with herself. There were always companies willing to hire data security specialists from the wrong side of the firewall, as long as they came with the right credentials, and Ilsa wasn't in any particular hurry. She had some money yet in her private accounts, and Kai would see her share of Dantes's fee deposited. She could certainly trust him that far, even if she'd given him no indication of where she intended to go.

The truth was, Ilsa didn't *know* where she wanted to go. No particular system or sector called out to her in moments like this. She'd been a wanderer far too long to think of any one place as home. As a child she'd been accustomed to living wherever her parents could find work; as an adult she'd crafted her own life the same exact way. Even before Kai she had been constantly in transit, usually to wherever she could accumulate more skills or equipment or deeper access to the data at her fingertips.

There was comfort to be found in a life on the move.

But everything was different now. She'd spent seven years growing accustomed to traveling with a partner at her back, and Kai's sudden absence proved disquieting. After three restless days, Ilsa caught herself looking for him in the crush to disembark.

Gantry Beta was a frenetic settlement in a border system. The messy quilt-work of a planet had belonged to no one until joint terraforming teams from six worlds crafted a breathable atmosphere out of its base components. It was the perfect place to land and catch her bearings. No one noticed or troubled her amid the anonymous chaos of species. Ilsa felt alone and unnoticed in the sprawling city that surrounded Gantry Beta's third largest spaceport.

She stayed for a month, all the while wondering if Kai would appear on her doorstep. Ilsa hoped and dreaded and wondered what she would say, but she was never able to come up with a sure answer. The memory of their conversation still ached—words she was painfully accustomed to, having heard them so often and from so many people.

She'd never expected to hear them from Kai.

Ilsa had made few lasting friends in a lifetime of constant motion. Self-sufficiency was simpler, and the truth was she found most people exhausting. Only a handful, a persistent few, had stuck around long enough to work their way past her instinctive defenses. All of them let her down eventually. Most wanted something more than friendship, and walked away when Ilsa wouldn't give it. Some left her on better terms, a natural parting of paths. None had ever *stayed*, and until Kai, that hadn't bothered Ilsa at all.

Until Kai, she hadn't trusted anyone enough to rely on them; now she knew what it was like to have someone stick around. Seven years. It was a completely different paradigm. No wonder she felt truly lonely for the first time in her life.

No wonder she was disappointed when Kai didn't appear.

By the time she left Gantry Beta, Ilsa had a job offer in the Prihe Cluster and a bank account freshly padded by the Roy Vis Medica Group payroll. She'd spent a month resisting the urge to look for Kai's footprints in the local data stream, and she left without giving in to curiosity. There was no point in knowing Kai's location or itinerary. She wasn't going to contact him, and she certainly wasn't going to return contrite to his side.

She boarded an Aian light liner without looking back, and set out to work the entirely legal side of data security.

There was no shortage of jobs after that initial jump. Ilsa had a skill set in high demand, and within six months she'd set herself up with her own corporate front and a new business account. Vance Security Consultations. Travel expenses almost always landed on the companies calling her in, and no job kept her in one place for more than a couple of months. She chose gigs based more on distance and duration than on pay. The wanderlust that lived beneath her skin had mounted to new heights, and instead of planets and cities, Ilsa found herself tiring of entire star systems. She felt more restive with every breath she took, and there was no one at her side to slow her pace.

Ilsa forgave Kai eventually. A year out. Two years. She realized the knot in her chest had loosened. She wasn't angry at Kai anymore. She missed him too much. Every ship she boarded had a stranger in the seat beside her where Kai belonged, and the wrongness of it all gnawed at her with dull persistence. She was painfully aware of the constant gap where her best friend should be.

She still didn't give in to curiosity or try to track him down. She recognized futility when it was staring her in the face.

Exactly three years after Eleazar Dantes, Ilsa Vance returned to Naius V. Pure chance brought her back to the planet where her final mission with Kai had begun. The Naiasuss Research Institute offered her a package too good to turn down. Their primary research hub was positioned on the farthest continent from the port city she and Kai had called home between jobs. She saw no reason to let sentiment prevent her from accepting the generous offer.

Besides, Ilsa chided herself, she couldn't let the past dictate her entire future. She and Kai had too much history for her to avoid every planet that reminded her of her absent partner.

So she settled in to a new job and a brighter city, relieved when she arrived to sleek streets that were entirely unfamiliar. Even the air smelled different, and at night there was no glimpse of stars through the powerful glow of city lights.

Ilsa worked hard for the Institute, even when familiar restlessness began to edge beneath her skin. She stayed buried for days at a time in her data screens, breaching security wherever she could in order to find the weakest points, then helping craft sturdier walls and smarter traps. It wasn't thrilling work, or even particularly challenging, but she was damn good at it.

Two weeks into her stay, she upgraded from the cramped room provided by the Institute to a private apartment several blocks distant. The neighborhood was quieter, the apartment larger, and she had enormous windows along two out of five walls. There on the twenty-second floor, high up from the street, Ilsa had a perfect view of the endless horizon.

She worked six days out of every seven, and on that seventh—her first day to herself in her new accommodations—she was startled by the tone that signaled a visitor at her door. It wasn't a communications alert from the building's main entrance, where any guest should have been held up by the security checkpoint. It was the chime of her own front door. Whoever this was had bypassed the building's security somehow, and the thought set Ilsa's nerves alight with warning.

She was already fully awake despite the early hour, dressed in a loose skirt and well-worn sweater. She'd wanted to watch the sunrise through the wide spread of her new windows, perched on the faded sofa that had come with the apartment. The chime nearly startled her into spilling her coffee. She set the mug on a small end table as she rose, and collected her gun from the end table's only drawer. She favored excessive caution over carelessness, and it was with quiet apprehension that Ilsa approached the door and reached for the control panel beside it.

She tapped the voice control and kept her tone cool. "Yes?"

"Ilsa, it's me." Kai sounded tinny through the cheap control panel, but there was no mistaking him.

Ilsa dropped her hand, severing the connection before her choked gasp could carry into the hall. Adrenaline rushed through her, bringing an incoherent mix of hope and panic. She set her gun down on the kitchen counter, and then jabbed her finger too hard at the control panel in her hurry to undo the lock.

The door slid smoothly open as she fell back a step, and Ilsa gawped at the improbable sight of Kai Othen standing in front of her.

He wore the same brown jacket he always wore. There was the same dusting of stubble along his jaw. He looked rumpled around the edges, as though he'd only just arrived planet-side and barely paused to rent a room before hurrying to her door. The too-bright sunlight from the windows cast him in sharp contrast and made him look like some kind of statue instead of a living, breathing man.

The sight of him sent relief spinning through Ilsa's blood, and she took another step back so that she could brace one hand on the sofa.

Kai watched her from the door frame for several seconds, but finally asked, "Can I come in?"

"Yes." She tightened her fingers on the faded cushion beneath her hand. "God, of course you can come in. What the hell are you doing here?"

Kai gave her a wry look, all exasperated fondness as he stepped inside the apartment. "I'm here for you. I hoped we could talk."

She let go of the couch and approached him cautiously. The door slipped closed at Kai's back, the lock automatically engaging with a quiet ping. She peered up at him, half expecting him to disappear as abruptly as he'd arrived. She felt silly needing the reassurance of contact, but she set a hand to his arm just the same. Ilsa exhaled slowly at the solid feel of muscle beneath his sleeve, sturdy and familiar. She closed her eyes and dropped her hand, drawing a steadying breath as she let herself believe he was actually here.

Ilsa gasped a small squeak of surprise when Kai's arms closed around her, crushing her in a hug that squashed the air out of her lungs. Her eyes opened, but she couldn't see Kai's expression. He had her wrapped too tightly, his face buried against her shoulder. When Ilsa managed to get enough leverage to return the hug, Kai's only response was to hold on even harder. He was shaking.

By the time he let go, Ilsa's chest had begun to hurt, and it was only partly for want of oxygen.

Kai took an apologetic step back, a sheepish expression on his face. He stuffed his hands into the pockets of his coat and watched her with a faint tilt to his head. He had the air of a child who feared he may have done something wrong but wasn't yet sure. Waiting for either anger or reassurance.

Ilsa took a moment to collect herself, but finally said, "You came back."

His expression clouded, his brow creasing at the center. "Of course I came back. We're partners."

She shook her head, denial and uncertainty transparent in the gesture. "No one's ever come back before."

Kai's face smoothed as comprehension overwrote confusion. He looked more at ease somehow when he confessed, "I'd've come sooner, but I wasn't sure you wanted to see me. Even now... I thought you might send me away, but I needed to try."

Ilsa's voice caught in her throat, a bundle of messy emotion nearly choking her. *I'm glad you're here*, she wanted to say. Or maybe, *Thank you for coming back*. The words wouldn't materialize, though. The sentiments lodged somewhere in her chest, and she turned her back on Kai, looking for some excuse on which to focus a sudden excess of energy. There was only the kitchen, with its narrow beverage pod at the corner of the counter still cued up, hot and ready.

"Do you want coffee?" She managed to ease the superficial question past the roadblock in her throat. "You look like you've been up all night, let me pour you a cup."

"Ilsa." Kai's voice was firm. Fond. Surprisingly patient.

She subsided but couldn't bring herself to turn around. Not yet. Not when she still didn't know *why* he was here. She didn't want to believe he was the kind of man who would track her down across the known galaxy just to make a second bid for her romantic affections. She knew him better than that. But people had let her down before. Ilsa wasn't sure what she would do if Kai managed to compound his mistakes.

"I'm sorry," Kai said, and Ilsa stopped breathing.

She turned her head, glanced back over her shoulder and let herself meet his eyes. He looked exhausted and sad and completely sincere.

"I'm sorry," he repeated. "I let you down, and I hurt you. It's taken me a while to work out how badly I fucked up, but I do get it now."

"Kai..." Ilsa turned at last, voice tapering to nothing.

"I took you for granted. I made assumptions. I said awful things." Kai's mouth turned down at the corners, and the hazel of his eyes darkened with regret. "I'll understand if you still want me gone. Say the word and I'll be on the next flight out." He paused, looking distinctly unhappy. "I already booked a seat, just in case."

The clench of feeling in Ilsa's throat released at his final admission, and a lighter sensation started twisting its way free. Pre-booking travel arrangements, before he'd even come to see her, was so perfectly, *typically* Kai that she almost smiled despite herself. He would never take the chance of someone calling his bluff if he couldn't deliver, so he'd covered all possibilities before reaching her front door.

It was without any conscious intention to answer that Ilsa heard herself say, "I don't want you to leave."

A heartbeat passed before Kai seemed to process the assertion, and then a grin spread across his face. It was a wide open expression, a relief so honest that looking at it made Ilsa's heart twinge. She felt one corner of her own mouth twitch upwards with relief all her own.

"I miss working with you," Kai admitted. "I want you back if you'll have me."

Ilsa sobered, wariness resurfacing. She caught the flicker of doubt in Kai's face at her change in demeanor, but she couldn't afford to blindly reassure him. She needed to know exactly what she would be getting herself into if she said yes.

"Are you still in love with me?" she asked, and then held her breath as she waited for an answer.

"A little." Kai gave a sheepish smile and a helpless shrug. There was an apology in the slouch of his shoulders. "But that's my problem. I'll get over it."

"I can't do this again, Kai. My feelings aren't going to change, and I can't spend the next five years wondering if I'm leading you on."

"Hey," Kai said softly. He took a step toward her, his tall figure looming close without touching. "Despite overwhelming evidence to the contrary, I'm not a total clod. I don't make the same mistake twice."

"And you're really okay with this?" Ilsa asked. "With going back to the way things were? You want to work together even knowing I'm never going to feel that way about you?" She willed him to say yes. She wanted him back so fiercely it hurt, but she couldn't accept a reunion on any other terms. She couldn't promise him more than she'd already given, and she sure as hell couldn't do this if they didn't understand one another perfectly.

"You're my best friend and my partner," Kai said simply. "That's all I've got any right to ask for."

They were at a crossroads, Ilsa realized. Two paths stood before her, entirely opposed, and only one of them included Kai. There was no halfway and no middle ground. She had to let him back in completely or let him go forever. Compromise would only tear them apart.

Trust was dangerous. It was an opening in vital defenses, a gaping vulnerability. It was the potential for fresh agony if he let her down, and Ilsa couldn't pretend the possibility didn't terrify her.

But trust was also a deliberate gamble, and Ilsa recognized the stakes. Kai wasn't a man to make empty promises. He watched her now with fierce understanding. It surprised Ilsa how easily she believed he would stand by his words.

"Okay," she said at last. "I'm in."

Kai's face split into a grin as wide and warm as the sunshine streaming into the apartment, and this time Ilsa found herself grinning back. Her chest filled with a bright, crisp hope, and she threw her arms around his shoulders. She had to stretch onto her toes to reach, and Kai laughed, wrapped his arms about her waist in return and lifted her easily off the floor.

Ilsa buried her face in his coat and smiled into the soft leather.

When Kai set her down he was still smiling, even as he retreated far enough to let her breathe. "I can probably buy a second ticket," he offered, mischief in his eyes. "We could get off this rock today."

"I have a job to finish first." She arched an eyebrow. "I can't just shove off in the middle of a contract. Aside from the ding my professional reputation would take, they still haven't paid me for my services."

"Right," Kai conceded reasonably. "Then I guess I'd better get my pack out of that storage locker and find a place to stay."

Ilsa didn't hesitate. "You can stay here. There's a second bedroom down the hall."

He blinked at her in surprise. "Are you sure?"

"Positive. Go get your things."

As she watched him disappear through the door, she felt giddy and lightheaded. Tranquil in a way that confirmed her choice. There was an easing in her spine, a soothing of the disappointment she'd carried with her since Praxica VI.

"Welcome home," she said to the empty room, and smiled so wide her face hurt.

FIN

ABOUT THE AUTHOR

Yolande Kleinn may be a shameless dreamer and a stubborn optimist, but she is also a proud purveyor of erotic romance. Excitable, fastidious and a little eclectic, she spends every spare moment writing the stories she wants to read. If she can drag other people into the pool along with her, then so much the better.

You can find Yolande via her website:
yolandekleinn.com

OTHER TITLES BY YOLANDE

AN INTIMATE CHARADE

Cargo ship captain Galin Odona is in desperate need of a contract. When a lucrative opportunity comes his way, he invites Addison Valdez—smart, stubborn, and the only Human member of his crew—to join the negotiation.

Anatoria Baell's contract is not precisely legal, and she has unconventional methods for choosing where to put her trust. Galin agrees to pose as a distant relation during a gathering at her private estate. The negotiation takes a complicated turn when Addison proclaims that Galin is not only his captain, but his mate. The hot-headed lie puts them in a tough spot, maintaining their charade for the duration.

But Galin is a terrible liar. Even worse, he's been in love with Addison for years. Now, through tight quarters and an illusion of intimacy, he must win the contract without giving himself away. The task seems monumental, but Galin cannot afford to fail.

EVERY SECOND YOU'RE ALIVE

Major Franklin Cade has spent years fighting the undead scourge that drove humanity from Earth. Now victory is in sight, but it's come at immeasurable cost. He has sacrificed everything in the line of duty—even his own heart.

For six months Lieutenant Daniel Mendoza has been missing in action. Only stubbornness and a refusal to tarnish Mendoza's memory have kept Franklin alive since losing the man he wouldn't admit he loved.

When a perilous rescue needs volunteers, he returns to the canyon where Mendoza fell. He is not prepared for the hope that ignites as he follows a fading distress signal across infested terrain. In the shadow of a deadly countdown every second is precious, but Franklin refuses to lose Mendoza again.

ASHES ON A DISTANT WIND

Before the Vrete came to Earth, Donovan Riggs was a man of faith. Now they're gone, and he's left that part of himself behind for good. In the ruinous aftermath of a war nobody won, he is simply trying to survive. With Beau Greer—a young medic who stumbled into his life and then refused to leave—Riggs travels dangerous roads between long-dead cities. Scavenging doesn't offer much of a future. It barely provides for the present. But Riggs will do anything to protect what's his.

SOMETHING BORROWED

When public defender Trevor Ortega finds himself dateless for his ex's wedding, faking a relationship seems like the perfect solution. Less perfect is his thoughtless impulse to invite Sebastian Greer—friend, federal judge, and former boss—as his plus one. It would be a solid plan if not for one problem: Trevor's been in love with Sebastian for years, and each fraudulent touch will remind him of everything he can't have.

Trevor doesn't know why Sebastian agreed to his scheme, but there's no backing out now. It's only one night after all, and what's a little heartbreak between friends?

www.ingramcontent.com/pod-product-compliance
Lightning Source LLC
LaVergne TN
LVHW091140080826
845145LV00008B/2212

9781946316394